Crackcoon

GARY LEE VINCENT

Burning Bulb
PUBLISHING

Crackcoon
By **Gary Lee Vincent**

Burning Bulb Publishing
P.O. Box 4721
Bridgeport, WV 26330-4721
United States of America
www.BurningBulbPublishing.com

First Edition.

Paperback Edition ISBN: 978-1-948278-61-4

Also by Gary Lee Vincent

Dedicated to
Brad Twigg

CHAPTER 1

These sorts of illegal meetings always took place in the same kind of nondescript locations; in this case, on this Thursday evening, in an alley.

The alley reeked of piss and other things that the two men currently entering it couldn't put a name to. It was on North 6th Street, of Glen Elk, a small warehousing district in the town of Clarksburg, West Virginia. One of the alley's walls belonged to a Chinese restaurant, the other belonged to a drycleaner's; but what was most important about the alley was that neither of its side walls held windows that were often opened, rather the windows on both sides both had bars on them and were kept shut around the clock. This was mainly because the alley had no lights at all, and neither business establishment was willing to take a chance on someone breaking into their building.

The time was about a quarter to eight at night. To avoid notice from the restaurant's customers, the two men were approaching the alley from the street that ran along the rear of the two buildings flanking it.

The two men were named Chris and Mo. Both were long time crackheads, the kind that had gotten so addicted to 'sucking the devil' as it was often called, that they'd long ago lost all respect for themselves. Neither man had a home anymore, they lived rough, crashing for the night wherever they could. Both wore clothes that had grown filthy from neglect, and their shoes had holes in them. Nothing really mattered for either of them except the drug they craved.

Chris was the older of the pair by about ten years. Mo hadn't been totally decrepit for long, but given time he'd be a lot worse than Chris; that was if he lived long enough to grow old naturally; and it was good odds that he wouldn't.

Both men peered cautiously into the alley; they squinted through its darkness to the parking lot at the far end where the restaurant customers parked their cars. The alley was empty.

"You sure he said he'll be here?" Mo asked Chris. He had the jones on him now; his last hit of crack had been two hours ago.

His older companion wasn't in much better condition than himself, but he nodded. "Yeah, yeah, he'll be around. You can count on Denny to show up once there's money."

"I ain't got no money," Mo said.

"Yeah, yeah, I know that," Chris said. "I already told you I'll take care of you. So long as that greasy bastard Denny shows, that is."

"Hey, here he is now," Mo said, with evident relief in his voice, pointing out Denny's car swinging into the parking lot.

"Yeah, speak of the devil," Chris agreed, his relief also audible in his voice. Denny Hallman was a reliable drug dealer. Chris and Mo had never had any hassles since they'd been copping from him.

But, as he approached them now, Denny Hallman didn't resemble the devil. Denny was tall and skinny, and very well-dressed in comparison with his two clients. And in sharp contrast to the two crack addicts' barely concealed desperation for their next fix, Denny's face showed nothing but greed.

Denny walked a short distance into the alley, to a point where he was largely invisible from the roads at both of its ends. After a short pause, Chris and Mo also stepped into the alley and walked over to meet him.

He smiled at the two men; his face just discernable in the dark. It was an obviously dishonest smile, but that was what the addicts all wanted; to be treated with respect, even though they didn't respect themselves. Denny was cool with that. Whatever it took to separate a fool from a dollar was fine with him.

"So-so-so, you got the stuff?" Mo asked, the shakes threatening to take him over now that their cure was so nearby. It was all he could do to not leap at Denny and attempt to beat him up (or even kill him) to score some rock; that white translucent compound that at the moment was more precious than diamonds to him. He was certain Chris felt the same way. But neither man would ever try that on with Denny Hallman. Denny might not look like much, he might not even be packing a rod, but there were rumors he was well-connected with the mob.

Even the motherlode of dope wasn't worth getting killed over.

"You got money, bro?" Denny asked in return. "You know I don't take American Express."

"Yeah, I got money," Chris said. "I got enough for what we wanna buy."

"Great, then let's talk business. How much rock you guys want?"

"A hundred bucks worth."

Denny's façade of respect slipped for a few seconds. "You two derelicts planning on throwing a party or ODing together?"

"Hey, man, we ain't here to be insulted," Chris said. "Are you gonna sell us some nuggets or do we have to ask elsewhere?"

Denny made a show of waving his hands at them. "No offence meant, fellas. But see, maybe regular crack ain't what you two connoisseurs need. Uh-uh, guys, ol' Denny here's got something different for you two tonight."

Mo looked at Chris before replying: "The fuck you talking 'bout, man?"

Denny laughed in the half-light. "Bro, I'm talkin' 'bout the latest thing to hit town. Agent Orange."

"Fuck that," Chris said. "I just want some regular rock."

"Yeah, we do," Mo agreed. "No bullshit."

But Denny wasn't about to be put off so easily. "Guys, guys, hear me out," he went on. "I'm still talking crack. Guys, this orange stuff is supercharged crack, stuff that guarantees you'll both get lit." In the darkness, Denny's body language now suggested disbelief. "You two telling me you ain't heard of this Agent Orange shit?"

Chris snorted. "Hey, I might be old, but I can still smell bullshit a mile away. What's the catch? This new stuff cost an arm and a leg or what?"

"No, no, don't'cha get me wrong," Denny said soothingly. "It's the same price as regular, but it's giveaway price now 'cos we're trying to introduce it to everyone." He laughed in the darkness. "You pay the same price as always and I'll hit you up with the new shit."

"Better not be no tricks," Chris said. "Money's hard to come by."

Mo nodded his quiet agreement to this.

"Don't I know it?" Denny agreed also. There was a moment's pregnant pause, and then Denny added, with a touch of impatience now, "So, what's it gonna be, guys? Regular or high-octane?"

Mo looked nervously at Chris, who slowly nodded back. "Alright, Denny, hit us up with it. But if it don't get us lit like you promise, we ain't coming back."

Denny laughed. "No problems there, dude. The orange shit don't blow your mind, I'll even give you a refund."

"It's that good?" Mo asked, with the start of excitement in his voice.

"Way better. Now let me see some money, or else I'll take my bizzness elsewhere."

Chris pulled five crumpled twenties out of his pocket and passed them across to the drug dealer. Denny counted the cash and then, after nervously peering left and right out of the alley to ensure no one was witnessing this transaction, he reached into his jacket pocket and pulled out a small baggie. Before handing the baggie over to Chris, he shone a penlight on the contents.

"Looks like orange candy," Mo said. "Li'l orange rocks."

"Yeah, even down to the powdery coating," Denny agreed, snapping off the flashlight and handing the rock cocaine over to his client. "But once you feel it, you'll know the difference." Then he laughed. "It looks like candy for a good reason. See, my chemist supplier ain't taking no chances. We don't want the pigs interfering before we flood the streets with this stuff."

CHAPTER 2

"You think Denny was bullshitting us?" Mo asked nervously as they made their way back to their current crash pad in an abandoned trailer.

"We'll find out soon enough," Chris replied. "But you heard how sure he was of himself. So, I'm sure this orange rock is good, just not as good as that li'l creep is making it out to be. He was just givin' us the hard sell."

They reached the trailer and entered it, and Chris switched on the trailer lights. Actually, the trailer wasn't really abandoned, but its last occupant had left a week ago, seemingly for part's unknown, and never being ones to let opportunity pass them by, Chris and Mo had since made themselves comfortable in the trailer.

Inconspicuously, of course, because of the neighbors.

Of course, once Joe the trailer's owner returned, they'd need to move on, but that happening was in the future and was currently just a vague possibility anyway. For all they knew Joe could be dead right now, or have been arrested for breaking his parole and returned to jail.

"You gonna share with me like you promised, aren't ya, man?" Mo asked with a wheedling tone in his voice. Now that he was so close to getting his high again, he couldn't shake the fear of his possibly being deprived of it.

"Sure thing," Chris agreed, dropping his dirty coat over a chair and then picking up a glass crack pipe from an end table. "But excuse me if I try it out first, to ensure that that motherfucker didn't cheat us and hand us real marshmallows instead of the real deal."

That sounded fair enough to Mo and he relaxed. Besides, he suddenly had an intense desire to piss.

Meanwhile, Chris felt around in his trouser pocket for the baggie of crack cocaine, and when he finally fished it out, held it up to the light for examination. He opened the baggie and pulled out one of the small orange rocks that it contained. "It looks like tiny marshmallows, but don't feel like 'em at all."

That said, Chris put the rock in the bowl of the crack pipe, flicked on his convenience store lighter and applied the flame to the crack. The vapor swirled and he inhaled.

Mo waited for his verdict. If that motherfucker Denny had sold them some crap, they'd be out hunting his ass and when they found him, they'd had his ass to him on a plate, mob connections or not.

But then Chris smiled stupidly. "Shit, dude, Denny wasn't lying. This stuff'll hit a home run on ya." He offered the pipe to Mo. "Wanna hit?" Then, like he'd just remembered something important, he flung the baggie over at Mo. "Here's yours. Hey, what you looking so ansty for?"

"I gotta piss!"

"So fucking go piss!" Chris growled at him. "What'cha waiting for? You expecting me to come hold your dick for you?"

Now, Chris was usually a mellow sort of guy, and now suddenly he had this weird aggravation in his voice. Mo tried to remember if Chris always got like this when the crack hit him; but the drug had fucked up his brain too badly now that he both imagined that was the case and wasn't the case also. In any case Chris had been as good as his word and had shared the crack with him.

Mo looked over at his own crack pipe, which lay on the same end table as Chris's had. Mo considered taking the pipe along with him to the bathroom.

Nah, he thought, *that'll be stupid. And I'm leaving the crack here as well. I don't wanna drop it down the shitter like we did that other time and were forced to have a dry spell for two days.*

So, Mo walked over to the table and placed the baggie on it.

"Dude, I thought you wanted to piss," Chris asked in that uncharacteristic pissed-off voice. "So . . . so what the fuck you still doing here in my damn living room?"

Chris was behind Mo and Mo wasn't looking at him yet. Mo was more concerned about placing the baggie somewhere where it would be safe, but also where it wouldn't go missing in the short time he'd be urinating. His bladder felt full to burst now, but he wanted to be certain he was hiding the orange crack rock where Chris couldn't get a hold of it, if he suddenly had a change of heart about sharing it.

"I'm talking to you, man!" Chris growled again in that uncharacteristic vocal tone that made him sound a lot like an angry bear. "Don't you dare piss in here!"

"Cool it, bro, I ain't gonna piss in here," Mo replied. "I'm on my way to the bathroom."

And he was. At least, he was on his way to the toilet until he turned around and got a good look at Chris.

Chris was no longer seated on the couch lighting up and smoking. No, the old guy was now standing directly in front of Mo, in direct line with the hallway door. He was still lighting up the crack pipe and toking from it, but each time Mo attempted to step past him he moved also to block the way.

"Hey, let me past, man, I really gotta go." But then Mo paid proper attention to his friend and what he saw now really scared him.

Chris was still the older decrepit man that Mo had grown used to over the past six months, a man in dirty clothes, with a dirty beard and a constant reek of unclean sweat coming off of him.

The difference was that both of Chris's eyes were now bright orange, completely orange, with no distinction between retina, iris or pupil. In fact, Mo quickly realized that Chris's eyes were as orange as . . .

Mo glanced quickly at the baggie on the table. *Hey, is it Denny's orange crack that's messed him up like this?*

"I thought I told you not to piss in our damn living room!" Chris screamed at Mo.

This statement made Mo realize that in his shock and fright over Chris's weird transformation, the urine in his bladder, tired of waiting for him to visit the bathroom, had drained out of him by itself.

"I'm sorry, man," he whimpered, suddenly realizing he was in danger.

"Sorry just ain't good enough, asshole!" the transformed Chris yelled at him and then struck him violently in the face with the crack pipe.

The pipe hit Mo in the left eye, completely pulverizing it. The eye exploded like a bomb and blood splattered out from it. Shocked by the pain and terrified now, Mo backed away from Chris. With one hand clamped to his face, he searched for a safe place in the living room. But both living room exits were on the other side of the room, and reaching them would mean getting past Chris, who was still lighting up the pipe and smoking its bloody content.

"I warned you, asshole!" he screamed then charged at Mo again, his bright orange eyes gleaming with rage.

Mo turned and tried to escape, but Chris was too fast for him. Like an angry bear, he bore Mo down to the floor, rolled him onto his back and began stabbing him in the face and neck with the crack pipe, cruelly tearing up his skin and flesh and violently shattering his facial bones until Mo finally gave up the ghost and seemed relieved to be doing so.

Then Chris stood up and looked around the room. By now, he was more-or-less completely out of his mind. He had only two desires, violence . . . and more of the wonderful orange rock. His desire for the former had now been satisfied for a while, but his craving for the latter, his need for the crack variant called Agent Orange, was only just beginning.

He looked down at his crack pipe, which was stuck halfway through Mo's neck, and gave it up as unusable. With his bright orange eyes gleaming with intent, he swiveled his head until he was staring at Mo's crack pipe and at the baggie lying beside it, which contained the rest of the cocaine rock.

Chris picked up the baggie and the pipe, retrieved his lighter from the floor, and then returned to the couch and lit up again.

Yeah, the high's even better than before, the crazed man thought. He glanced over at Mo's corpse. *Too bad that damned idiot had to go mess up our trailer by pissing all ov—*

It was exactly at this point that Chris' brain, bombarded with conflicting signals from this new superpowered crack variant, overloaded and then shut down. He jerked for a while as he died, pissing himself too, and then falling limp sideways on the couch, with his lighter and the crack pipe spilling to the floor.

But Chris's eyes still seemed to be on fire. His eyes still shone bright orange in his face when the paramedics, alerted by a neighbor who'd been alarmed by the shouting and commotion in what was supposedly an empty trailer, broke down the door and found the two stiffs.

CHAPTER 3

Blissfully unaware of the deadly effect of the new drug he was peddling, Denny Hallman drove his old blue Cadilliac SUV through the outskirts of Elkins.

Denny felt good this evening. His was generally a shifty existence. Dealing drugs wasn't any kind of a great career, it was survival living.

How could one expect to build any kind of a future when one had the constant hassle of the pigs sniffing down one's neck? One bust— doing time for dealing, or for possession with the intent to distribute— and you were as good as cooked. Once law enforcement had you logged in their books as a drug dealer, they'd never stop hassling you.

What kind of a life was that to have?

Not a good life at all, Denny thought. *Not when you're small fry like me. But this time I'm about to score big, and then Las Vegas and Hollywood, ya'll better darn watch out, 'cos Denny's coming to blow ya'll wide open!*

With happy thoughts of skimpily dressed showgirls in his mind, Denny noticed a raccoon crossing the road. Being the nature-loving sort of guy he was, Denny immediately swerved his car to avoid hitting the raccoon.

"Hey, rat, you better watch the hell where you're goin'," Denny yelled at the startled animal as he rolled past it. "Someone else might not be so careful!"

Denny looked back in his interior rearview. The raccoon was still standing in the middle of the road. It seemed perplexed by its narrow escape from death. *Maybe the thing has a death wish like goddam lemurs,* Denny thought.

A short while later his phone rang. Denny checked the screen. It was Max, his chemist friend. With a grin on his face, Denny immediately forgot about the raccoon, and placed the phone to his ear.

"How're sales going?" Max asked. Like all chemists, Max had a nervous kind of voice, one that was in this case made even more nervous by the fact that he was involved in a criminal enterprise with Denny Hallman, who, truth be told, couldn't be considered the most reliable of partners. But in reality, Denny was the only criminal scumbag Max knew, so Max had to work with him.

"Sales are good, bro," Denny replied. He liked Max because Max had brains and was about to make both of them super-rich.

"Any reviews yet? I mean from our customers," Max asked nervously.

Denny made a turn before replying. "Not yet, bro, but they'll come. You know, we just began pushing the stuff last week. It's selling like hot cakes though, that's for sure."

"Yeah, yeah," Max readily agreed. "But how about repeat orders, we should be getting some of those by now. That Agent Orange stuff is fucking potent—I mean, I coded 'addiction' into it that's worse than a junkie's craving for heroin."

"Oh, yeah, we're getting lots of repeats," Denny said. "It's just that . . . Hey, hey, bro, that just reminded me. I need to stop by your lab for a new batch of shit. At the moment I'm on my way to the Sleepaway campground. I just realized that I don't have enough Agent Orange on me. So how the hell am I supposed to sell it then?"

"The campground? What're you going to do over there?"

"More business, dude. There's sure to be a lot of folks at the campground who might like a little 'candy' to spice up their weekend, if you know what I mean."

"If you say so, man."

"So . . . have you got any more Agent Orange ready? I need enough for the whole weekend."

"Yeah, sure," Max said. "Got a new batch fresh out of the cooker. Come over now if you like. Make sure you bring the cash 'cos I gotta settle my suppliers too."

"Be right over, bro."

Denny hung up. Like he'd just enlightened Max, he'd been on his way to the camping and hiking trails in the nearby mountain, but now he pulled his SUV over to the shoulder. After waiting for a truck to roll past, Denny turned the blue SUV around and headed back to town.

On the way, he saw that the raccoon he'd almost hit a while ago had now left the road.

Oh yeah, Denny really did feel lucky now. This new orange modification of crack cocaine that Max had cooked up—Agent Orange—was sure to revolutionize the drug business. And like all good businessmen, Denny Hallman was in on the ground floor.

It was simply the gravy train from here on—up, up and away. Denny could already visualize a rain of cash showering down on Max and himself.

CHAPTER 4

As though they desired to continue their fatal friendship beyond the grave, the corpses of Chris and Mo lay side-by-side on mortuary tables in the Harrison County morgue. Mo had no eyes left, but both of Chris' eyes were still wide open and staring, and were only slightly less orange than they'd earlier been.

The county coroner Lewis Smith was talking to his assistant Jerry Oldman. Both dead men had already been autopsied and stitched up again. The main concern had been to discern the cause of Christopher Mason's death. How Moses Jones had died was obvious.

"So, that's two more fatalities related to this new brand of crack cocaine," Lewis told Jerry. "Making a total of four now, but those other two were ODs like this one. The orange transformation of the eyes is a clear indication of usage, but not in all cases. In those other two related fatalities we examined, the corpses' eyes were only slightly discolored with an orange tint. He tapped Chris's shaven head and ran his latex-gloved fingers down to the man's eyelids. "This gentleman, however, looks like he stuffed little oranges in his eye sockets.

Jerry, a young bespectacled man, nodded as he regarded the two corpses. Despite his undeniable fascination with Christopher Mason's abnormally colorized eyes, his attention was more drawn to Moses Jones's head, which was a huge mess. No amount of postmortem plastic surgery was going to be able to fix this; the dead man would clearly be having a closed casket funeral.

"I still can't understand, why he kept hitting him," Jerry said. "He must've known the guy was dead for like ages, and yet . . ." Jerry looked away from Mo's body—the sight threatened to make him puke. Not the violence of his death—after all, Jerry was a mortician—but the sheer randomness of the violence, the unnecessariness of the amount of physical damage that one man had inflicted on the other. He gestured at the dead man's face, which was distorted by holes, several of which inexplicably penetrated all the way through the skull. "It's crazy that he kept stabbing him with the crack pipe even after he was long dead."

Lewis nodded sagely. "I agree, but there's the effect of designer street drugs for you. Kid, we both read the toxicity report the lab boys sent over." Lewis sighed. "This new street drug has the addictive qualities of crack combined with the uncertain nature of 'bath salts.' Lewis paused and laughed. "And I know you know I'm not referring to the damn things cleaning you out from the inside."

Jerry smiled. He knew all about narcotic 'bath salts.' "That's fucked up big time," he said. "Boss, did you hear about that incident down in Miami, where that guy on bath salts ate another person's face off?"

Lewis nodded. "Yeah, the woman was his girlfriend. She was on salts too, died at the hospital from sheer shock. I guess her death was inevitable. The crazy sonofabitch ate her face right off, right down to the white bone; ate all of her skin and flesh off, chewed it up, and swallowed it down like it was rare steak." He frowned at his bespectacled assistant. "And now, it would appear that this new street drug is just as dangerous. Crack only half drive you crazy, but this orange stuff"—he tapped Chris's shaved dome—"it takes you all the way to the asylum."

"Sooner the cops get a handle on it the better," Jerry said. Or else we're gonna have our hands full in here."

"Worst thing about it, is how unpredictable this stuff is. According to the lab boys, there's no way of predicting who's gonna go nuts from usage. No telling at all."

"Or who's gonna die either."

With that grim thought in mind, the two men rolled the two dead men away into cold storage.

And while they did so, Jerry Oldman couldn't stop looking at Mo's head. What sort of insane rage could make one person do that to another person?

Jerry was relieved when he shut the door to the meat locker on the gruesome sight.

CHAPTER 5

Gary Bentley stood outside on the front porch of his house and stared at the woods. It was Friday morning, and the time was approaching noon.

Forest ranger Gary Bentley was a tall man, both tall and large, with short dark hair that included both a mustache and beard. He was generally calm, except when bad things interfered either with his family or with the forest, both of which he loved passionately.

Gary had been married to Charlotte Bentley for twenty years now and the couple had a nineteen-year-old son Mike who was currently in college in Penn State, studying marine biology. Gary sighed whenever he thought of Mike. He'd always hoped that any kids and Charlotte had would share their love of the forest and its wildlife, and would in turn become forest rangers also; just as his own father and grandfather had been, a family tradition that dated back to the beginning of the twentieth century.

But sadly, that seemed not to be the case with Gary's own offspring.

Looks like the forest ranger tradition in our family is going to die out with me, Gary thought as he surveyed the woods opposite the front porch. Then he laughed and said aloud, "Well, pa and Grandpa, we had a good run, but like they say, all good things gotta come to an end sometime." Gary laughed some more, the sound appearing to fill the morning. "Yeah, Mike ain't just embarking on a career outside of the forester life, he's taking on one that will ensure he never has anything to do with trees in his life."

"Hey, leave our kid alone," Charlotte admonished from behind Gary. "He got his own life to live."

Still laughing, Gary turned around to face her. "Yeah, I know that, lady. It just gets to me sometimes that he doesn't share our love of the trees and the animals. What exactly do fish have going for them that forest creatures don't?" Gary pulled Charlotte close and kissed her warmly on the lips. "Why, for instance, can't he share your love of raccoons?"

Charlotte Bentley, tall and slim and blonde, laughed. "Oh, honey, I think it's the raccoons that are driving the boy out of the forest."

She said this only half in jest, and Gary wisely did not comment on it.

Charlotte's love for animals, raccoons in particular, had long been a sticking point between them. It wasn't something that they quarreled over, not anymore at least, but in past years it had fueled many an argument between them.

But nowadays, Gary tried to be more accepting of Charlotte's opinions.

In this philosophical spirit, he nudged Charlotte gently with his elbow and said, "So, what really brought you outside now, hon? Has Elvis gone missing again?"

Elvis was Charlotte's 'pet' raccoon. Insomuch as a wild animal could become domesticated, Elvis was a domestic animal. Like a dog or a cat, Elvis came and went as he pleased, and Gary had resolved his reservations about having Elvis (and any other raccoons Charlotte adopted) in the house by regarding him as a sort of funny-looking dog. Not so Mike apparently, as the kid had raised hell the last time he was home on finding Elvis sleeping in his bed. This has been particularly comedic as Mike had invited his girlfriend home that weekend, and apparently the reason Elvis had climbed into bed with them was to investigate what they were doing under the covers that was making so much noise.

But the raccoon was generally harmless and was easy to tolerate, which made Gary wonder why Charlotte now looked so worried about it.

"Hey, you didn't reply me, honey," he said. "Has Elvis hurt himself?"

Charlotte shook her head, "No, that's not it. But I mistakenly left the fridge door open when Elvis was in the house this morning and he got into the fridge and stole the last pack of lunch meat and ran off with it. So, there'll be no sandwiches for you to take off to work today, honey."

For a moment it seemed like Gary was about to lose his temper. Then he let out a long sigh, and forced himself to smile at Charlotte. "See, what I've been talking about, baby. I've always told you that it's not wise to familiarize wild animals with human beings as it creates all sorts of problems. Now that little thief has deprived me of my sandwiches."

At first Charlotte looked displeased also, but then she burst into loud laughter.

"What's so funny, woman?" Gary joked. "You know I run on my belly."

"I'm sorry, but it's not that," Charlotte said. "I'm just remembering Mike and Lisa finding the raccoon in bed with them."

Gary first looked at her like he didn't know what she was talking about. But then the memory came to him too and he also burst out laughing.

"Yeah, that sure was something," he agreed. " 'Cuz at first I thought someone had died in there."

Arm-in-arm, they laughed for a while longer on the porch, and then Charlotte abruptly left Gary's side and walked over to the right edge of the porch.

Gary's curiosity as to what had taken her there was soon answered. A raccoon was peeking through the pet door Charlotte had had him build into the side of the porch screen over on that side so her little friends could easily get in an out.

However, Gary's slim hope that it was Elvis returned in penitent mode with the stolen lunch meat in tow was quickly laid to rest when the raccoon peeking through the pet door climbed fully through it and approached his wife.

This raccoon was not Elvis; this one was female and quite pregnant.

"Oh, Lisa, where have you been?" Charlotte asked the animal, bending down to pat her on the head. The female raccoon accepted this good-naturedly, but not without casting suspicious glances over at Gary, whom she seemed to distrust.

I think it's my ranger uniform they can't get used to, Gary reasoned, looking down at his clothes. *The animals must be used to seeing me in the woods by now, but for some reason I still represent a kind of danger to them.*

"Come come come inside, little woman, and let's get you some lunch," Charlotte was meanwhile exhorting the raccoon.

With Lisa following cautiously because she was still not used to being inside the house, Charlotte entered the building.

Gary watched the two of them go with great amusement.

No wonder the kid opted for marine biology, he thought. *What do you expect when his mama named a raccoon after his girlfriend?*

CHAPTER 6

By the time Gary was about to set out for the ranger station in his pickup truck, two more adopted raccoons were also having lunch in his kitchen.

Gary sighed at the thought that the creatures were supposed to be sleeping now, but had grown so used to his wife feeding them in the daytime, that they'd become largely diurnal, rather than nocturnal like God intended them to be.

"Hey Joe, you really mustn't eat so much sugar or you get all hyper and shit," Charlotte chided one of the male raccoons.

Yes . . . shit indeed. Gary remembered this as one of the other reasons he preferred leaving raccoons in their natural environment. Over the years he had endured at least fifteen incidents of his wife's pet raccoons using their front porch for their latrine site.

Gary sighed. And the problem with raccoons was that they didn't defecate in random places like dogs or rabbits did. No, once those little animals found a toilet spot that they liked they kept reusing it.

Gary checked that he had his car keys on him and then addressed Charlotte, who was occupied with pouring food from various cereal packs into bowls for her raccoon guests, along with little portions of chopped up nuts and fruit. "Okay, honey, I'm off now."

She looked up with a smile on her face. "Okay, honey, be careful out there in the big bad woods."

He nodded. "I will, hon, tho thankfully these are peaceful parts, and the campers and bears hardly ever make a nuisance of themselves."

"Well, just be careful anyway," she insisted "you never know what's out there."

Then, feeling one of the raccoons tugging at the pack in her hand, she returned her attention to the animals again, but not without asking over her shoulder where Gary would be driving today.

"Oh, pretty routine, I'm going to be working the back of the mountain, then swing by the cabins for a bit and finally check out the Sleepaway campground to ensure that they're not getting too rowdy back there. Then finally, back to Ranger Station to log my report for the day." He bent down and kissed her cheek. "All in all, I should be back in time for dinner." He was working an afternoon shift today that would end at 7 p.m.

"All right, honey, but once again, be careful?" Charlotte replied.

Gary grunted a reply to that, and hurried out of the house. But at the front entrance he turned and looked back again, staring long and hard at his crouching wife and at the raccoons she was feeding.

For some reason, although it seemed ridiculous to consider, Charlotte's repeated request that he be careful had stirred in Gary Bentley the unpleasant feeling that today wouldn't be the piece of cake he'd anticipated. Stranger still, the feeling of danger seemed to hinge around raccoons; or one raccoon in particular, that missing little lunchmeat thief Elvis.

The apprehensive feeling lasted only a few seconds. After which, telling himself not to be silly, Gary Bentley walked down the porch steps, climbed into his forest ranger pickup truck and set off along the mountain road that led to the ranger station.

CHAPTER 7

"Yeah, man, this is the life," Tom Jackson told the others late that Friday evening as he lifted open the trunk of his car. "All we're gonna do here this weekend is have fun, fun, fun!"

"Well, I certainly hope so," his girlfriend Sara Grimes said, with a pout. "I gotta ease down after the stressful week I've had at work.

"Baby, we should have never left college," Tom told her. "The real world just puts a damper on the fun life, ya know?"

His three young companions laughed.

"But, dude, we needed to grow up and become responsible adults," Marie Komar said.

"I like the adult part, but who the hell needs responsibility?" Marie's boyfriend Ron Nicoles told her, while pulling her close for a squeeze.

Tom and Sara had been dating since high school. No one had expected their romance to survive past prom night, but somehow it had, continuing forward into their college years, till now they'd both graduated and it seemed inevitable to them both that wedding bells would ring for them at some point in the future.

Tom worked in IT, while Sara was a receptionist for a local car dealer. On the other side of things, Ron was in-between jobs and Marie had just quit being a waitress to return to school for postgrad studies in Social Service.

The four of them had been planning this trip for two months. The trip had been hard to set up because, aside from the differing schedules of their jobs, Tom and Sara were the only two who lived in the town of Elkins. Ron lived in Morgantown and Marie was now enrolled at far off Liberty University in a different state.

The Sleepaway Campground occupied the west side of the Stuart Recreation Area on Kelley Mountain. It was a well-frequented location to which folks travelled from all over the state. It was well organized too; in addition to open areas were folk could pitch their tents as they liked, the camp also had cabins for rent.

From here in the camp parking lot they could see the Shavers Fork river, which lay at the end of a short trail. They were maybe a quarter of the way up the mountainside, on an area where the ground leveled off for a mile or so. All around them were trees and behind them lay the road that led back to the state highway. Up beyond this campground area, the lovely green countryside continued.

"Okay, guys, gimme a hand here," Tom said, pointing to the huge drinks cooler, that occupied a third of the space in the rear of his Kia Sorento.

Ron stepped over and took hold of the cooler's far grip. Together, the two friends hefted the cooler out and set it down on the grass.

"That's a lot of alcohol," Marie said.

Ron was immediately at her side, leering over her shoulder. "That, baby, is because we plan on doing a whole lot of drinking, partying . . ."

". . . And other things like exploring you two ladies' thongs," Tom finished, making Sara and Marie both roll their eyes. Then he snapped his fingers. "Okay, vacationing ladies and gents, let's inventory everything."

Ron began counting off on his fingers. "Okay now, we got beer, tents . . ."

"Music and food . . ." Sara added. "Our camping clothes."

"Water," Marie filled in.

"And hot babes to make it all worthwhile," Tom said.

The 'hot babes' jointly sighed at that comment, and then Sara asked, "Boys, how about marijuana?"

"Yeah, dudes," Marie said, staring at Ron with a meaningful stare. "You guys were supposed to buy pot, enough pot to turn this weekend vacation into a 4:20 affirmation."

"So, did you get it or not?" Sara added, with an equally meaningful stare at her own boyfriend. "Are we getting high this weekend or not?"

"No," Tom said with a sad look. "We didn't get any drugs."

Sara and Marie both looked at their boyfriends in disbelief.

"What?" the two young women jointly shrieked.

"Calm down, sexy ladies," Ron said.

"Don't you dare tell us to calm down," Sara growled. "How the hell can you guys screw up like this?"

"Baby, the weed was supposed to calm us down," Marie added.

"And now, we don't have any weed, so we're just gonna be stressed-out bitches to you both all through this weekend," Sara said philosophically. "Well don't blame us then."

"Please calm down a moment, both of you pretty ladies," Ron said. "Tom hasn't gotten through telling you everything yet."

Marie scowled at him. "What? There's more to this lack-of-recreational-medicine fuckup?"

Tom nodded. "We don't have the drugs here because we couldn't pick them up earlier in the day 'cos of work, and afterwards because of all that last-minute shopping we had to do. You girls know the sort of rush we were in to hit the highway before it got dark." He smiled. "But, girls, our recreational medicine is already been paid for. Denny's gonna deliver them here to us."

"Yeah," Ron added. "In a short time from now, we'll have coke and pot to spare."

Sara lost her look of desperation and smiled. "Oh, that's okay then."

Marie nodded. "Yeah, you guys could have explained things better and not scared us like that. Because I for one, am really looking forward to getting drunk and high." She winked at Ron. "And gettin' laid too, of course."

Sara gazed expectantly at Tom. "Just how soon is this guy Denny gonna arrive?"

Tom looked up at the sky over the parking lot, down towards the state highway, and then checked the time on his wristwatch. "He should be getting here about as soon as we get through setting up our stuff at the campsite."

"Let's get to work then," Sara said impatiently, then she sighed. "Wow, you guys, this is a lot of stuff to carry."

CHAPTER 8

The sun was about midway low in the sky, falling fast towards nightfall, and Denny's blue Cadillac SUV was cruising the highway, heading for the Sleepaway Campground. This time Denny wasn't alone. His companion was a woman named Tess Diaz, who was, simply put, a hooker.

Tess was a redhead who was well-stacked everywhere; lots of tits, lots of ass, lots of leg; which in her profession equated to lots of male customers.

Tess was also halfway to becoming a crackhead, which was why she consistently hung around Denny, who dealt in the stuff. Denny didn't hold her moral failings against her; in fact, he approved of Tess's weaknesses, as they meant he could get laid as often as he desired. All he had to do was flash the lure of a great high at Tess and she'd come running with blowjobs on offer.

And he'd flashed that lure at her today. Once he'd shown her the pouch containing the fresh batch of Agent Orange he'd gotten from Max yesterday, she'd been willing to visit hell with him if necessary.

As was normal when they went on similar outings, Tess carried the drugs. She had a big purse, and even though she regularly stole stuff from Denny, he pretended not to notice. She never stole much, so Denny saw no point in making a big deal about it. Today her purse held some cocaine, regular crack in addition to Agent Orange, and a large quantity of marijuana.

"Denny, I don't understand how the hell you intend to sell all of this weed at the campground," Tess said, while Denny steered the car through the many twists and turns that comprised Route 250 at this point. She patted the handbag. "It's a hell of a lot of marijuana."

Denny laughed. "Relax, baby. I've already gotten a buyer for most of that weed. This guy I went to high school with called Tom? Well, he called me a week ago, said he'd be up here in the woods with six friends, and they'd need to get high. He wants to get high?—I told him I got him covered. He was supposed to collect his stuff earlier in the day, but couldn't make it over, so I offered to deliver—for additional gas money, of course; I don't run no charity gig. The coke is for their crowd too, though he said no to the crack."

"All this stuff is theirs? They must be quite rich then."

Denny laughed. "Oh, they ain't broke." Then he looked away from the wheel for a moment and frowned at her. "And, oh yeah, once we meet 'em, no trying to drum up any business. You're solely mine this weekend."

Denny felt it was important to drum this info to Tess's ears, otherwise she might vanish to advertise her wares the moment they arrived at the campground.

"Yeah, yeah, I got you, Denny," Tess said, running her tongue over her red lips. "So long as the rock's good, I'm all yours for the weekend." To drive home her point, she dipped her hand into his crotch, found his manhood and squeezed it hard. Denny instantly got hard and almost lost control of the car; he just managed to get it back under control before he veered across the double yellow line.

Thanking God that there'd been no cars approaching in the other lane just now, he said: "Hey, take it easy, girl. What'cha tryin' to do? Kill us both?"

Tess flashed him a smile. "I'm just showin' you how grateful I can be once my needs are taken care of." Then she faked a pout. "But the rock has to be as good as you claim, or I won't be very good to you either."

Denny wheezed in relief. Now he realized their close shave with disaster had been even closer than he'd thought. Looking in the rearview mirror, he saw a cop cruiser pull into view behind them.

However, the pair of officers didn't seem to have their attention on him. The cop car wasn't speeding up or anything and their lights hadn't suddenly begun flashing, and so Denny Hallman resigned himself to their having a police escort for the next mile or so until he reached the camp turnoff.

Shit, man I gotta be careful.

"Girl," Denny calmly told Tess, who hadn't yet looked in the rearview and seen the cruiser behind them, "just you wait till you've tried Agent Orange. You'll never, ever wanna leave my side, 'cos I've got the direct hotline to heaven."

Tess frowned. "You keep hyping up this Agent Orange shit. Is it that good?"

"Baby, just wait and see. Once you've sampled Agent Orange, you'll rate it higher than anything you've ever used before."

They were getting close to the camp now, climbing the mountainside at a slow pace, which Tess imagined was because Denny wanted to enjoy the splendor of the countryside, but which was really because Denny, conscious of how much narcotics he had in the car with him, and of how much jail time those narcotics would fetch him if the police found them, was being careful not to attract any suspicion.

In a sense, Denny Hallman was very aware that he was leading a charmed existence. He'd been dealing hard drugs on the streets of Morgantown for five years now and not once had a policeman ever stopped him and insisted on checking his trunk.

Such a run of such extremely good luck is certain to switch to extremely bad luck sooner or later. That's just the law of Karma. He smiled, aware that Tess watching him. *This is my big chance—I better not screw it up. By my calculations, if Max keeps producing Agent Orange at his current rate of production for another two months, we should have saturated this county and be ready to move to the nearby counties . . . Hmm, but Max is worried about how we're ever gonna succeed in laying low then. Also, he's already worried by what happened to Chris and Mo, wants to wait and refine the product a little more. But I told him those two were just fuckups. They most likely mixed Orange with heroin or something.*

"Hey, there's something I was gonna tell you about," Tess said.

"What?" Denny asked after a glance at the rearview revealed that the police cruiser was dropping behind them again. He hoped that maybe they'd gotten word from Dispatch about a felony being committed somewhere else; hopefully across the county.

"Well," Tess explained. "This dude at the county morgue, a good customer of mine, he told me like they brought in these weird-looking stiffs with bright orange eyes."

Denny glanced over at her. "Bright orange eyes? What's that? Another sexually transmitted disease?"

Tess shook her head. "They think it's a brand-new drug. But they don't know what it—shit, Denny, look out!"

Denny had been staring at Tess and not looking at the road. Now, as she screamed, he looked back and saw something in the road. A raccoon, a fucking raccoon.

Not again!

Not very interested in adding to the amount of roadkill on American highways, Denny swerved the car to the left to avoid the raccoon. He just managed to avoid splattering the raccoon, and pulled the car back over the double yellow line again, by which time the damned misplaced animal had vanished into the forest.

But after straightening the car out on the road again, Denny heard a noise behind him that made him glance in the rearview mirror.

He groaned. The police cruiser behind them had just activated its siren, and its lights were flashing. Denny immediately knew what the problem was. Contrary to his previous reading of the situation, the officers in the cruiser must have seen him lose control of the car when Tess had grabbed his crotch and had been watching him since then, not desiring to pull him over except he showed actual signs of driving under the influence.

"They're pulling us over," Tess said, now noticing the cruiser.

"What the hell are we gonna do?" Denny said miserably. He could already see himself in jail, getting buttfucked night after night, and all because of a stupid raccoon.

At the moment he felt like making raccoons an extinct species. Raccoons must really have it in for him. This was the second time in two evenings that members of their evil animal tribe had tried to commit suicide via his car. If the damned things desired to die so much, why couldn't they simply wait for a drunk trucker who'd be sure to make burger patties out of their hairy little asses? Why the hell did those evil creatures have it in for him? He now wished he'd splattered the damn raccoon instead of swerving to avoid it. And the one yesterday also.

The police car had increased its speed to catch up with Denny; but so far, because of a sudden uncharacteristic stream of vehicles in the oncoming lane, the officers hadn't been able to pull him over.

"Hey, I've got a plan," Tess said.

"What plan?" Denny asked desperately, already feeling the big boot of the law being shoved up his backside.

"Keep going and speed up," Tess said, pointing forward. "We're already at the camp turnoff. Listen, once we make the turn, the cops won't be able to see us for a few seconds. So, I'll throw my handbag into the forest there. We can come back for it later."

Denny immediately sped up the car and turned off the highway. Just like Tess had predicted, the tall trees bordering the turnoff entrance shielded them from view for a few seconds, precious seconds that Tess expeditiously used to throw her narcotic-packed handbag as far into the woods as she could.

She had just enough time to settle back in the front passenger seat before the police cruiser once more showed up in Denny's rearview mirrors. Here in the tree-shadowed tunnel formed by the huge trees on either side of them, there was no escaping the cruiser's loud siren.

"Keep going," Tess told Denny. "Don't stop yet."

"It's okay," Denny told her. "We're far enough from the junction now that they won't suspect what we left behind."

Sighing audible sighs of relief that he wouldn't be going to jail any time soon, Denny pulled the car to the roadside and waited for the police cruiser to reach them.

CHAPTER 9

Tess's disposal of her handbag hadn't been as unnoticed as she and Denny thought.

Taking a leisurely stroll through the woods after erecting their tents, the quartet of Tom, Sara, Ron and Marie were almost reaching the campground turnoff, when they saw the dark blue SUV pull into the sideroad.

Tom, Sara, Ron, and Marie were still a distance from the road and not easily visible between the trees.

"Well, it looks like our pot just arrived," Tom said on recognizing the car.

But then Sara, who was holding hands with Tom, shook her head. "I think your guy Denny has some trouble. Look!"

The four of them watched as Tess flung her handbag out of the car window. The purse traveling in a majestic slow arc before descending out of sight amidst the far-off trees.

"Maybe he had some heat on him," Ron said, as the police cruiser entered the campground road also. The cruiser's flashing lights and siren left no doubt that they were in pursuit of the blue SUV.

"In that case, they got rid of it just in time," Sara said.

"Okay, everyone into hiding," Ron said. "We ain't criminals, but there's no point in putting ideas in the lawmen's heads."

"Yeah," Tom agreed. "Particularly when we know the guy they're chasing."

Everyone then stepped a bit further into tree cover, so they could watch the road without being seen themselves.

"I doubt Denny would be carrying a gun," Tom said. "It's likely just our drugs they're so desperate to offload." He laughed and jabbed Tom with his elbow. "Dude, that was a whole fucking lot of Mary Jane we ordered from the guy."

"And with coke too? Hahaha! Yeah, dude, I'm sure Denny was already seeing the number of his jail cell before his lady friend disposed of the evidence."

"Hey, baby, enlighten me," Sara said. "Why won't Denny have a gun on him? I mean, *we've* got a gun with us."

"Huh?" Marie asked in surprise. "We do?"

"Yeah, yeah," Ron informed her, kissing her on the ear. "I brought mine along. Just for safety. One never knows what kinda creeps one might run into in these kinds of out-of-the-way places. Or bears too. There aren't supposed to be any around here. But then, in my opinion at least, one can't play it too safe in the woods."

"You know, that does make me feel a lot safer," Marie said, turning and kissing Ron back.

The police cruiser was now approaching Denny's vehicle, which had already pulled over to the side of the road and parked.

"And to answer your own question, honey," Tom told Sara, "carrying a gun is more problematic for criminals. If the cops search the car and find it, they'll check its registration. And most crooks will have an unregistered firearm on them, one that can't later be traced after being used. If I'm right, that's quite illegal too."

"Well, either their illegal gun or our illegal pot is safely hidden somewhere amidst the trees now," Marie said, laughing. "Making the trees accessories to criminal activity. Sooner or later the police will leave and then we can get started on having fun."

"I can't wait," Ron agreed with her. "If the guy gets arrested, we know the general area where his girlfriend threw her bag. We can retrieve it, keep what's ours, and return the rest to Denny later."

That made lots of sense everyone, and so they all settled down patiently to await the outcome of Denny Hallman's encounter with the police.

CHAPTER 10

The four friends who'd been walking through the woods weren't the only ones to witness Denny's desperate disposal of his drugs.

There was one more witness. True, Elvis the raccoon did not see Tess throw her handbag out of the car, but he saw it sail through the air a mere ten yards away and watched it crash against the base of the tree it hit.

Being a small animal, the raccoon's immediate response to both missile and impact was response to a perceived threat, and this resulted in Elvis taking to his little heels and finally ducking out of sight behind a tree.

In normal circumstances too, the raccoon, which could hear the sound of people speaking at two different locations not too far away, would then have moved on to what he considered a safer part of the woods at this point in time. But something stopped Elvis from leaving.

A smell. A strange and yet strangely familiar smell was coming from the strange missile that had fallen out of the sky to the base of the tree. The smell attracted Elvis like a magnet. Elvis knew that smell. He quickly associated it with the giant hairless female creature that lived in the wooden burrow about a mile away. The giant creature was very friendly and often shared her food with him. And this smell coming from the white object that had fallen a short distance away reminded Elvis of one of those edibles that the giant creature had shared with him, those small round orange nuts that tasted sweet like oranges on the outside, and were soft and nutty on the inside. Try hard as he could, Elvis had never been able to find the tree that produced those tasty orange nuts anywhere in the forest.

So now that their smell was coming from the thing that had fallen just a short distance away, it was natural for the raccoon to disregard any potential danger and head over there to investigate.

***

Elvis reached Tess's bag without either accident or incident. The bag was open, its magnetic clasp having come undone on its impact with the tree, and so the raccoon found it easy to sift through the mess of contents.

He quickly found what he was looking for, the small plastic bag packed full of those small orange nuts that he loved. Okay, so the smell wasn't exactly the same, but it was close enough for the little raccoon, which, suddenly startled by the noise of the police cruiser starting up and reversing a short distance away, quickly pulled the plastic bag of orange nuts out of the handbag, snapped it up between his teeth and then ran off to safety amidst the trees. The package's intoxicating smell in his nostrils seemed like a dream accomplished to Elvis.

Only when he was at a safe distance and out of range of any immediate interference from the giant hairless creatures did Elvis place the package down and begin to examine its contents.

CHAPTER 11

The police cruiser pulled up behind Denny's SUV.

There were two police officers in the black and white cruiser. Once they'd parked their vehicle, both officers pushed its doors open and got out.

"We're in luck," Tess said, as she glanced in the rearview. "The guy on the left, Chomski, he's a good friend of mine. Don't know his friend tho'."

By now Denny was feeling at ease. And so, he smiled at the cop who leaned in at his car window. This was the officer that Tess didn't personally know. The cop's face was hard and cold, like he didn't have time for DUI shit like this.

"What happens to be the problem, officer?" Denny asked respectfully.

"Sir, your license and registration please."

Knowing he couldn't afford any hassles with law enforcement, Denny always had those documents properly up-to-date. He handed them over and the cop looked through them and handed them back to him.

"Okay, so what was that driving stunt you just pulled back there, swerving across the road like a maniac?" the man asked after giving Denny back his papers. "Sir, I can smell your breath. You don't smell like you've been drinking, so I ain't gonna order a breathalyzer on you. But what was that all about?"

Denny shrugged. "There was this raccoon in the road and I swerved to avoid flattening it."

The cop nodded. "Yeah, that does happen a lot up in these mountain parts. Okay, sir, I'll give you a pass for that one. So, now,

I've got another question for you? How about the first time you lost control of your car? Was that another raccoon? 'Cos if you say it was, sir, I'm throwing your ass in the back of that cruiser and hauling it down to the station."

Faced with that threat, Denny decided to come clean. It was embarrassing, but what else could he do? So he gestured over at Tess, who was waving out of her own window at the second policeman. "Well, she was . . . you know . . ."

"No, sir, I don't know," the cop interviewing him said. "What I do know is that in the short space of about five minutes, you've twice endangered human lives by your reckless driving. Now what was that first incident about?"

Denny was saved from replying by the cop on Tess's side of the vehicle calling out to his companion: "Hey, Joey, over here for a minute."

"Coming, Pete." Joey left Denny's side and walked over to Chomski. The two chatted for a short while beside their cruiser, with Chomski pointing over at the car and laughing. Finally, Joey nodded and both officers walked over to Denny's car again.

When Joey looked back in Denny's window, he had a look of amused disgust on his face.

"Alright, get lost, both of you," he told Denny, with a broad wave of his hand. "And no more shenanigans on the road."

"Hey, Tess, next time you grab a guy's dick, make sure it's in the bedroom," Chomski told Tess, who stuck out her tongue at him, and then pulled up her skirt, revealing lots of creamy thigh to both cops.

The two cops walked back to their car, climbed in and reversed out of the turnoff. In a short while they'd vanished from view.

Denny looked over at Tess, who was laughing quietly.

"You fucked that cop Chomski before, right?" he asked. "That's how he knew you grabbed my dick."

At first Tess neither confirmed or denied the accusation, but kept on laughing. Finally, she said. "Actually, I gave Pete a blowjob in his car one night while he was driving. He almost ran off the road twice.

And when he came . . ." She burst into laughter again, unable to continue her tale.

Denny sighed and then nodded. "Okay. So yeah, now that the danger is past, let's go retrieve your purse and get the hell down to the camp and dispose of the drugs," he told her, and then put the SUV in reverse towards the start of the turnoff.

CHAPTER 12

"Hey, dude, what happened just now?"

Denny, imagining that maybe the cops had planned a sting operation for him, almost turned to flee, but then he recognized one of four young people who were stepping out of the woods towards him.

"Tom? What the fuck are you doing here?" he asked.

"Technically, we were looking for you," Tom replied. "But that's not really accurate. Actually, we were walking through the woods when we noticed you pull into the camp turnoff. Then we saw her—"

"My girl Tess," Denny said. "She occasionally helps me out with business."

"Yeah," Tom went on. "We saw Tess throw something out of the car window."

"We thought of going to check it out, but then the cops pulled in here too, and it seemed best to everyone to lay low until they'd left again." This time the speaker was Tom's girlfriend. Sara, Denny thought her name was, though he wasn't certain. The other guy and girl in the group also looked familiar, like they'd all attended high school together. Oh, yeah, the girl was Marie something-or-other.

"So, dude, you got our stuff?" the second guy asked. Try hard as he might, Denny couldn't recall the guy's name. Until he introduced himself: "By the way, dude, I'm Ron Nicoles; we all went to University High together. I used to buy pot from you all the time back then."

Tess pointed a bit deeper into the woods. "Your stuff is in the handbag I threw out of the car. Did you guys notice where it fell?"

Sara shook her head. "Not clearly, we were closer to your car than to here, but," Sara pointed up near the highway, "it seemed to have landed somewhere over there."

"Well then, everyone, we'd better search for the life of the party," Tom announced. "Everyone pick a direction in that general direction and start looking."

"Not everyone," Denny pointed out. "Someone needs to keep a lookout at the junction in case the cops come back."

He looked at Tess, but she shook her head and replied, "It's my purse. I'll recognize it easier than anyone else."

"I'll do it," Ron said and walked off towards the turnoff entrance.

The search for Tess's purse continued for longer than anyone had anticipated, but finally Sara called out that she'd found it and the others crowded around her.

"Oh, yeah, and now we can all get happily stoned," Tom said, handing Denny the requested delivery money and accepting in return from him both the packed bag of marijuana and the slimmer, but just as packed baggie of cocaine.

"Oh, yeah, the party's about to begin," Sara agreed. "I can't wait to light up a joint and relax out beneath the stars."

Tom and Denny touched fists. "Now, Denny, if you and your lady Tess would be so nice as to drop us four back up at camp again—"

"Hey, Denny, the Agent Orange is gone," Tess called out in an alarmed voice. "It ain't here."

"Agent what?" Tom and Ron both asked simultaneously, with their girlfriends looking bemused also.

"It's a brand-new synthetic kind of crack," Denny patiently explained. "Or maybe, it's crack mixed with something else—I don't really understand the cooking process but the end result comes out orange, hence the Agent Orange moniker. But, bro, the high from it is like nothing you've ever experienced before. I didn't tell you about it 'cos I know you ain't into that shit." Then he lowered his voice and whispered, while jerking a thumb at Tess, who was agitatedly searching through her purse. "But the crackheads totally love that shit."

"Hey, I can't find it!" Tess almost screamed at them all. "It's not in the bag."

"Well, none of us have it," Denny told her. "We'll have to search for it again. It must have fallen out of your bag when you flung it from the car."

"Hey, we'll help you search for a while," Tom offered. "What does this Agent orange drug look like?"

"Like little bits of rock candy, or tiny marshmallows, 'cos they also seem to be dusted in the powder that flakes off of them in little amounts. But what you're looking for is a small bag about this size." Denny gripped his right hand in his left and then positioned them both so that his four right fingers were sticking out of the arrangement. "Yep, a bag this size filled with orange candy."

"Orange like prison convict uniforms," Tess added, with a worried look at Denny.

"That should be very hard to miss," Tom said. "Alright, guys, don't spread out this time. If the package fell out of the Tess's handbag when she threw it, it should be lying in a direct line with the road."

With Tess directing traffic, everyone spent the next ten minutes searching the forest floor for the missing drug package. The light was already fading and they turned on their flashlights or camera lights to search. The profusion of lights created a fresh worry in Denny's mind. If those cops came back and caught them in this activity, there was no telling what they'd think.

Denny felt relieved when Tom finally called a halt to their searching.

"Sorry, dude," he told Denny, "but I don't think that stuff's here in the forest at all."

"Yeah, maybe it slipped down somewhere in your car," Sara added.

Denny accepted that this was reasonable. And with the light fading, Tess was forced to admit it too. At least Denny assumed that she had.

"Hey, come on you, guys, I'll run you all down to the camp like you asked," Denny said.

"Yeah, that's a great idea, Sara quickly agreed. "I've done my fair share of walking for today."

"Me too," Marie seconded. "All I wanna do now is have a swim in the river, have some food, and get as high as a kite."

Denny nodded. "Let's go then," he said.

Laughing and joking, they all walked out of the forest. But when they arrived at the blue Cadillac SUV, they discovered they were one person short.

"Where's Tess?"

Denny looked around and realized it was a valid question. Tess was nowhere in sight.

"Tess! Tess!"

No answer.

Denny sighed. "You guys wait here; I'll go get her. She's most likely accidentally emptied her purse all over the forest floor."

That said, Denny stepped back into the forest to find Tess. As he parted his way through the leaves looking for her, he hoped she'd not tripped over a branch and knocked herself out, or worse. Losing their stash of Agent Orange was bad enough; Denny didn't want to have to visit the ER tonight.

But Tess wasn't injured. She was still standing at the last place Denny remembered seeing, by a tall maple tree, and was looking around with a scowl on her face.

"Babe, what's the matter?" Denny asked.

Tess didn't reply. Not until Denny grabbed her by her arm and shook her, did she slowly look around and seem to notice him. Denny was taken aback by the 'involved' look on her face. She looked weird, almost like she was stoned, which Denny knew was impossible, because they'd been together since noon, and . . . and all the drugs were still in the bag slung over Tess's shoulder.

"What's the matter with you?" He tugged on her arm. "Come on, everyone's waiting at the car."

"It's around here somewhere; I'm certain of it," was Tess's reply.

At first Denny didn't understand what she meant, but then he did and his lips set in a firm line of irritation. "What? You're still looking for that Agent Orange we lost?"

Tess nodded eagerly. "It's around here somewhere, I can smell it."

That really surprised Denny. "What do you mean—you can smell it?"

Tess almost looked about to explain, but someone yelled from the road, "Hey, you two, get your damn pants back on and get back here!"

"You can fuck at the camp!" a girl added.

Denny looked from Tess to the road, and back at Tess and then shrugged. "Whatever, babe, you can tell me later." He gestured their way out of the trees, and when Tess still seemed reluctant to proceed that way, grabbed her arm and pulled her after him. She went meekly, but unwillingly.

"Such a shame to let it go to waste like this," she said as they proceeded between the trees."

"For fuck's sake, give me a break!" Denny snapped at her. "We'll come back for it tomorrow. But even if it's lost, so what? There's lots more where that came from."

"I was just so looking forward to trying out Agent Orange tonight. You know, after you've raved so much about how great it is."

They were in sight of the SUV now. Everyone except Marie was seated in the car.

"Listen, babe," Denny told Tess, "Don't'cha worry 'bout it. I'll still hit you up like I promised. Tonight, you can do the regular rock, and if by tomorrow we still can't find that missing pack of Agent Orange, I'll drive back to town to get some more from Max. Either way, you'll have a cool weekend."

After saying this, Denny gave her an expectant look. The last thing he needed was for Tess to start sulking and refuse to sexually service him over the weekend. Being in a group that included hot girls was sure to give him lots of boners and he needed Tess to handle those erections for him, so he didn't make a fool of himself, or worse still, start trading his expensive drugs for sex.

To his relief, she nodded as they stepped out of the forest. "That's fine, Denny. It's just—" She sighed. "It's hard to explain, man, but I mean it, I can smell that damn missing Agent Orange nearby. It's an impossible odor to forget or miss."

Her words meant nothing to Denny, who saw nothing exceptional about Agent Orange's odor. He didn't recall its smell anyway. For a dealer like him, the orange compound's smell was just one among many.

And . . . in a smelly environment like this one—we're in a forest, for Chrissakes—how the hell can she claim she can smell the damn thing nearby?

"Hey, are you two gonna get in the car, or do we move our campsite over here for you?" Sara asked.

"Sorry, guys, I got a little caught up in a thing," Tess apologized and got into the car beside Denny, while Marie squeezed in the backseat with the others.

Denny started up the car and they set off down the road to Sleepaway Camp.

Yes, the six humans departed in their blue automobile, blissfully unaware that big trouble was brewing nearby.

CHAPTER 13

Tess had been right in saying that the missing Agent Orange was still nearby.

Behind a tree a short distance away from where Denny's car had been parked, a formerly innocent young raccoon named Elvis was busily filling his little stomach with the drug dealer's missing stash of Agent Orange, which he'd stolen entirely because the drug's smell reminded him of the orange candies Charlotte Bentley had once fed him as a special treat.

True, Agent Orange in no way tasted as nice as Charlotte's orange candy, but this difference soon ceased to matter to little Elvis, as within a few seconds the raccoon had become completely addicted to Agent Orange.

And that was just the beginning of Elvis's troubles. Even as he grew more and more addicted to this strange orange substance, Agent Orange was already working strange and devastating changes in his body and mind, turning him into something nature never intended him to be.

Soon Elvis had eaten all the Agent Orange that his belly could contain. There was still much of the orange candy-like substance remaining in the package, and not wanting to lose it, the raccoon dragged it off somewhere safe and stashed it for later retrieval.

And then, feeling suddenly inexplicably tired (as night was normally a raccoon's daytime), Elvis lay down and fell into a deep, if short, sleep.

And while he slept, those same crazy changes continued occurring in his body and his mind.

So that by the time he awoke again, Elvis the raccoon was a very crazy and dangerous little animal indeed.

CHAPTER 14

Gary Bentley had been checking things out for about four hours now. It has been a routine tour. There were three other rangers at the Stuart Recreation Area forest station, and patrol assignments were rotated on a weekly basis. A large part of the rangers' work consisted of keeping an eye out for fires and things (or people) that could start them. None of these men needed reminding of how disastrous a single blaze could turn out to be if left unchecked.

Which was why Gary always paid special attention to both the campground and the nearby mountain cabins. Most of the cabins were empty but their construction was mostly from ancient and dry wood and even a lightning spark could set them ablaze. That was the theory anyway. Gary was glad that so far neither he nor the other guys at the station had a chance to prove this theory either right or wrong.

At the moment Gary was driving up to the Sleepaway camping grounds. The campground was several acres wide and was bisected by the Shavers Fork river over which sat two sturdy bridges. Lots of trees, lots of wildlife.

Great place, Gary thought, as he steered the pickup truck along the slightly uneven road. Being a man who appreciated nature to its fullest, he enjoyed being alone on the road like this, with just the wind, the trees and the sky for company. There was just something pure about the countryside; something that washed the stress out of a man.

That was how Gary felt anyway. And those campers he spoke to generally said the same thing, that being out in the outdoors revitalized them like a shot in the arm, and that when they returned home after those weekend campouts, they felt like new people, reinvigorated to tackle life's headaches afresh.

Gary smiled as he parked the pickup truck. Yes, the weekend's camping had already begun. There were already three cars in the parking lot.

Gary alighted from the pickup truck and looked around. Everything looked normal, and so he set off down the east campground trail.

Almost immediately he found a bitter taste in his mouth because of the litter. Someone had upended seemingly an entire bag of empty beer cans into the forest at the side of the trail.

Why the hell can't people follow simple instructions and use the trash cans we set out for them?

As far as Gary could tell, it was a question without an answer. Oftentimes, humanity puzzled him with their perverse ability to do the wrong thing, even when doing the right thing was simple. He wondered what excuse the people who'd dumped the beer cans he was staring at would give if questioned.

Most likely that they were drunk at the time, he thought sourly, shaking his head. The pile of cans did look like the remains of someone's party.

He tidied up the beer cans as best he could, and made a mental note to have them collected and disposed of later. Then he resumed his walk, occasionally pausing to stare between the trees, checking for tents and campers. Just like the other, western campground trail, this one also led down to the river, only it arrived there by a much longer route.

Finding nothing amiss by the time he reached the river, and seeing no further sign of irresponsible littering like with the beer cans, Gary decided to check out the cabins. Though all of the cabins were on the opposite river bank, most of them were closer to this bridge than to the western one, which was why Gary had walked this way in the first place. From here, once he crossed the river, he could survey the line of cabins in five minutes, and then make his way westward to inspect the pair of cabins over there too.

So, Gary crossed the bridge. As expected, everything was fine. The cabins all looked exactly the same as they had the last time he'd seen them, meaning old and empty.

With that settled, Gary checked the time on his watch.

Almost time to be heading back. I promised Charlotte I'll be back for dinner. If I leave now, I can check in at the station and still make it home relatively early.

With long strides, he set out for the far bridge.

As he walked alongside the river, he thought of his son Mike and laughed.

Marine biology eh? Yeah, that's a great escape route.

The distance to cover to the other bridge was just about a quarter of a mile and soon Gary had reached it, or rather he'd reached the first of the pair of cabins by the bridge, the other one being on the other side of it.

Looking across the river from here he could see the parking lot and the cars in it.

No changes there, though the parking lot cars looked like toy models from this distance; still the same four vehicles as earlier: his own ranger truck, a dark blue SUV, and a white and a red sedan.

One difference, however, in his general perspective of the layout of the trees and the mountainside, was that from this vantage point across the river, he could now see better into the forest areas of the campground. Unlike before, when he'd been on the east trail and looking in, he could now make out two camping sites, each one identified by the colored triangular shapes of several tents.

Squinting between the trees, he managed to make out a male and a female shape at the farther of the two camp sites which lay somewhat back along the river. The man and women over there appeared to be in the process of breaking camp, having collapsed their tent.

Gary saw no one at the nearer camp, which lay almost opposite his present location, though its tents were set up fifty or so yards in from the river. This nearer camp had a barbeque grill, but it was well-situated, in open space away from the trees and was yet unlit.

Making a mental note to check back here tomorrow morning to ensure the campers weren't becoming a fire hazard, Gary returned his focus to the cabins.

Because this first one was situated right beside the bridge, he walked all the way around it. The locks weren't good on the doors and campers used it all the time if they didn't feel like setting up in the forest. That was fine with Gary and the other rangers. The cabins belonged to the campground, and except for about five of those downriver, the town authorities weren't too strict about people using them. Gary's job here and now was simply to ensure they weren't being used for anything that might create a fire hazard. True, most of these cabins stood away from tree cover, but he knew from experience that, borne on the wind, one small spark could travel a hell of a long way.

So, Gary dutifully paced round the cabin. He expected to find no problems and his expectations were being met. He was pleased by this, and had no intention of climbing either the cabin's front or rear porch steps and taking a look inside. The last time he'd been unwise enough to do this, he stumbled on a drunken couple having sex on the old living room rug; he wasn't sure who'd been the more embarrassed by the meeting.

That had to have been me, he smiled in memory, *as those two were so drunk they'd—hey, what's that?*

On first glance 'that' appeared to be more litter, stashed in a small nook hollowed into the rear of one of the wooden poles that supported the front porch.

Gary sighed and decided he'd better head over to both camp sites across the river right now and read the campers the riot act concerning littering. *If ya'll wanna live in the city, then live in the goddam city. Don't bring your trash and trashy ways here!*

Yeah, most likely those campers weren't the ones who'd dropped this plastic nonsense here, but Gary could still warn them against doing their own share of dirtying up his nice, pristine woodlands. He wasn't looking forward to doing so, and Charlotte was certain to be angry if he was home later than he'd promised to be, but today in particular, littering had gotten his goat and he wasn't in much of a mood to overlook the offence.

But on bending a little closer to what he'd noticed beneath the porch, it struck him as being oddly familiar.

Oh, my dear God, you gotta be kidding me, he thought on pulling out the half-empty lunchmeat pack. *Elvis was here?*

Once Gary got a good look at what remained of the lunchmeat, there was no doubt in his mind that their little thieving raccoon friend was the one who'd stashed the pack here for later collection. First off, the trademark on the plastic was Kahn's, the exact brand that Charlotte always bought because she knew he was partial to the spices in it. Secondly, the uneaten edges of meat were an untidy line of bite marks of the sort that Gary had grown familiar with over the years.

So yeah, Elvis had been out here. Looks like he'd left the building at the moment, but he was certain to return shortly for a fresh performance.

But way out here? The sheer distance from the Bentley's own cabin gave Gary pause for thought. How had the raccoon gotten out this far? But then he quickly resolved the matter. It was simple enough.

As the crow flies, our home ain't really that far away through the woods. It's just when I'm driving that it takes a while to get around.

That resolved, Gary got out his cellphone and took some snaps of the package for Charlotte and he to laugh over later. Once he'd done that and put his phone away, he stuffed the meat pack back in Elvis's hiding place. No point spoiling the raccoon's fun.

It was while he was admiring the little space where Elvis had chosen to stash his booty (which was totally invisible if observed from the front of the cabin), that Gary noticed the second pack with its orange contents. This was half-buried beneath a mound of leaves.

Gary pulled it out and sighed. *Oh no, damn Elvis has gotten himself some candy again!*

He picked up the pack and examined it closely. Yeah, for sure it was candy, looked homemade too. The candy was bright orange in color, translucent, and had a powdering of pale candy dust. He smelt it; unlike regular candy, it didn't smell particularly appetizing. Not desiring to taste any raccoon spit, he refrained from tasting it.

Gary got up from his crouch and held the plastic bag up to the fading daylight.

Now, this here is the sort of thing I'm always warning Charlotte about, he thought in mild anger. *I've told her to stop feeding the wildlife, but no, she's always giving the damn raccoons candy to eat; M&Ms and whatnot, and see now, Elvis has begun stealing other people's stuff too!*

Feeling quite indignant, Gary Bentley left the cabin and walked off towards the bridge. He carried Elvis's candy with him, seeing no great loss if the raccoon missed it on his return. In fact, he figured he was doing the raccoon a favor by taking the candy away from it.

At the very least I'll have saved the little fellow from rotting his teeth, Gary thought as he walked over the bridge. But primarily he was taking the orange candy along as evidence to confront Charlotte with.

He was already driving off in his ranger truck when he remembered his previous resolve to go talk to the campers about littering. He burst into laughter.

Yeah, that would have been funny, seeing as Elvis was responsible. Well, he wasn't the one who piled up all of those beer cans, but I'll talk to the campers about that tomorrow, maybe.

CHAPTER 15

Darkness fell and the night moved on slowly.

So far, the campout had been fun. Everyone was doing their best to get drunk as quickly as they could. The weed Denny had brought over was literally the best. The coke was good too.

Everyone however demurred at trying some of Denny's crack cocaine, and with good reason. Tom, Sara, Ron and Marie all had good lives, they had good jobs and good future prospects, and they all knew exactly the sort of effect crack cocaine had on its users. Once they got sucked into its circle of addiction, it was as bad or worse than heroin and only a few degrees better than crystal meth. If they were fools enough to start using crack, in a few months tops, everything they'd slaved for over the years, all those years studying in college, the student loans and all, could be flushed down the drain, and that bright and happy future all of them now envisaged would be spent counting the minutes in rehab.

So no, everyone had politely demurred to try the crack.

As a further cautionary point, Tom had quickly pointed out to all his friends how Denny wasn't smoking any of the rock cocaine himself, but was sticking to drinking beer and smoking reefer like they were.

Tess, however, had gotten a glass crack pipe out of her bag and had lit up. She seemed oblivious to the damage she was doing to herself.

Still, everybody had fun and got very high. They told campfire tales for a while, and then, as the night progressed and the weather lost some of its warmth, they split up and hit the tents; Tom and Sara in one and Ron and Marie in the other. Tom's married older brother Jake was supposed to be joining them along with his wife Nina, but so far they'd no-showed, though Tom had assured everyone that the pair, who were coming over from Marlington, were nearby.

Denny and Tess didn't have a tent, but that proved to be no problem either. Neither of the two cabins across the river had viable locks on their doors and as both were empty, Denny and Tess moved into the one almost directly opposite Tom and his friends' campsite. The other cabin, which was a hundred or so yards farther along the riverbank, was considered too far for one to walk to when one was both drunk and stoned oneself, and one's hooker girlfriend was tripping on crack fumes.

So, everyone was well set up for the night.

But it was going to be an evil night for a lot of them, though they had no way of knowing that at the moment.

CHAPTER 16

Gary Bentley got home from work and showed Charlotte his cellphone photos of the missing lunch meat and told her where he'd found it. They both laughed heartily over that.

But then Gary mentioned also finding some orange candy in Elvis's private stash, and then relaunched his old schtick about Charlotte not feeding the 'wild' animals:

"Listen, honey, Elvis and his kind are not designed by nature to eat sweets. If he gets used to them, they'll simply rot his little teeth. And seeing there's a campground nearby, he's gonna have lot of opportunity to find sweets in the trash."

"Humans aren't designed to eat sweets either," Charlotte retorted.

"True. But we have dentists and they don't. So, hon, please, stop feeding the damn raccoons."

But Charlotte had no intention of stopping. Gary was often away for long hours and the raccoons she'd domesticated were like little children to her, particularly now that her own son was grown and far away at college. Okay, so the woodland critters had no concept of the sanctity of personal property and if you left the fridge or pantry open with them in the house something was certain to be missing afterwards, but . . . Charlotte knew she'd be incredibly lonely without those lovable little animals in her life.

But Gary waved the bag of candy at her as proof of his being right.

"Just look how much this is," he said, waving the bag of orange candy at her. "Just imagine if Elvis had eaten all of it," he proclaimed, which in turn forced Charlotte to snatch the bag up when he put it down on the dining table, and examine its contents more closely.

"Gary, this ain't candy," she pronounced after licking one of the little orange marshmallows. "I think it's some kind of drug. A designer drug perhaps."

But Gary wasn't in the mood to accept any excuses or alternate explanations from her, and he insisted that he was right.

"No, it's candy!" he exclaimed, banging his arm on the table and making the dinner plates leap up in the air. "Don't try to fool me. That is candy, and for Christ's sake, woman, stop feeding the damn animals!"

Charlotte let him win the argument.

CHAPTER 17

Jake and Nina Jackson pulled into the Sleepaway Campground parking lot at about 10 p.m. Everywhere was dark now.

"Well, sweets, once again we're the last to arrive for the festivities" Jake calmly announced as the headlights of their car picked out both Tom's and Ron's vehicles already sitting parked at the edge of the grass.

"But considering the distance we had to drive to get here it couldn't be helped," Nina said in a soothing voice. "And I for one am really looking forward to this alone time for both of us."

She leaned over the gear shift and kissed her husband on the cheek. Jake turned and kissed her on the lips, then said, "And I'm looking forward to catching up on all that ass you've been promising me."

Nina giggled. "Hey, it's not my fault that you're never at home during the week. Some weekends too."

Jake laughed. "Oh, I ain't blaming you, sweetheart. But I do intend to catch up on all the loving I've been missing; and without the kids interfering."

"Speaking of kids, I'd better call Rhonda to make sure they're okay."

Jake made a face. "See, there you go again. The kids are already starting to interfere with our weekend together."

Nina sighed. "Oh, don't be angry. I can't help it. I'm their mother."

Jake turned off the car engine. "Yeah, and I'm their dad and they're currently with their aunt and uncle and cousins; and so I say, leave our three little brats alone until tomorrow. They're sure not to have grown up before then."

Nina looked like she'd be angry at Jake's words, but then she burst out laughing. "Careful, man. If anyone else hears you say that they'll think you're serious." She leaned over and kissed him again, then pointed to Tom's car. "Come on, baby, let's go find your brother and his friends."

They got out of the car and retrieved their backpacks from the trunk.

"Too late to set up our own tent tonight," Jake said, gesturing down at the luggage packed in the trunk. "We'll have to share with the others, and get properly set up in the morning."

"We'd better call Tom and ask him to describe where they're camping," Nina said, shrugging into her backpack. Once she got it comfortably up on her shoulders, she flicked on her flashlight and gestured around the parking lot with it. The lot was deserted except for their car and the two belonging to their friends. "From here, everywhere looks exactly the same," she said, sweeping the flashlight beam over the trees and so creating a moving swath of green amidst the general black.

"No need to ask," Jake said. "I remember the directions from his text message. They'll be camped down by the river. Tom said to follow the trail on the right side of the parking lot until we reach the river. Then we walk left alongside the river till we reach the first set of tents, which will be theirs."

"That's simple enough," Nina agreed. "Should be impossible to miss."

And so, because Jake Jackson did not recheck the email his brother Tom had sent him and so didn't realize that the directions to the camp site actually instructed him to take the left trail not the right one, and then walk to the right instead of to the left, he and his wife Nina set off in the wrong direction.

Ordinarily their going the wrong way wouldn't have been too problematic or traumatic, but tonight there was trouble nearby.

**

"You know, maybe we're going the wrong way," Nina said after a while.

"Nah, I think we're still good."

"I just don't think it was supposed to take us this long to reach the river."

"Okay, sweetheart, you may have a point there. I for one, can't see those guys carrying all their luggage this far."

"So, what do we do now?"

But before Jake could reply to that, Nina had grabbed his arm nervously. "Hey, did you hear that?"

"Hear what?" Jake stopped walking and listened. "I don't hear anything."

But Nina was insistent. "I heard a sound in the woods, among the trees."

Jake laughed. "Darling, we're in the middle of the forest and it's the middle of the night. Don't you think the woodland animals will be going about their business now?"

But Nina wouldn't be persuaded so easily. Still holding tightly on to Jake, she turned around and swept her flashlight beam slowly along the lines of trees flanking them on both sides.

"Are you serious?" Jake asked her in some exasperation. He would have loved to make light of the situation some more, but the grip she had on his arm, with her fingernails digging painfully into his skin, convinced him that she was really spooked and scared; and slowly her fear was being transmitted to him.

"Okay, what exactly did you hear?" he asked.

Nina turned from raking her flashlight beam across the nearby trees to stare up at him, her face pale in the emerging moonlight. "It sounded as if someone or something has been following us," she explained in a voice brimming with anxiety. "That's what has gotten me on edge; not the fact that I heard a noise, but the fact that I didn't stop hearing it afterwards as we kept on walking."

She felt relieved that she had finally gotten her point across to Jake, because now he looked as concerned as she did.

"Okay, no point taking any risks," Jake said. "I think we better hurry on to the camp and hope we reach it quickly." He pushed her gently forward in the direction they had been going.

"Wouldn't it be better to return to our car?"

"It would have, if we'd just started walking. But we can't be far from Tom's camp now. So I suggest we proceed."

"Okay, so long as we walk fast."

And so, they hurried on, with Nina holding on tightly to Jake now.

Soon however, they both had to admit that they were lost.

"How far can it possibly be to the fucking water?" Jake spat, and then remembering exactly why they were now in such a hurry, he turned to his wife. "That odd noise. Are you still hearing it?"

She shook her head. "No, it's stopped now." She played her flashlight across the grass and trees around them. "But, darling, where are we?"

"I think we stepped off the right trail onto the wrong one at some point and never realized it. I also think we've walked ourselves away from the river instead of towards it. I'm assuming that if there was running water nearby, we should be able to hear it by now."

Nina was still holding on tight to him. "So, what do we do now?"

Jake sighed. "What I should have done in the first place: call Tom and ask him to confirm the directions to their location. Not that I think it will make much difference now."

Nina waited while Jake got out his phone and dialed, concentrating on his cellphone's bright screen instead of her own anxiety.

Because, all of a sudden, she could hear the strange noise nearby again. It was the sound of a small creature running about at the foot of the trees. She knew she was only assuming that the creature was a small one, but this was because the sound it made was coming from low down, close to the forest floor, and not higher up as she thought the noise of a bear or human being would do. By now she really wished that her husband could hear the sound too, so that she would know she wasn't going mad.

What was most upsetting about the sound was its randomness, the way it started and stopped as if the creature making it was in a manic state.

Oh, I hope it's not a rabid dog or fox that's been following us, Nina thought. *I don't want to get bitten and have to take rabies shots. Fuck, we really should have brought a gun along!*

"I can't get hold of Tom," Jake announced, his voice jerking Nina back into their immediate problem. "His phone keeps going to voicemail."

"Try his friend then. What's the guy's name again?"

"Oh, you mean Ron? Yeah, I've got his number somewhere too." Then he sighed. "That guy is a pothead. I just hope he's not zonked out of his skull now."

Then, noticing how nervous Nina still seemed, Jake asked. "What's the matter? Honey? Have you begun hearing the strange noise again?"

She nodded nervously. "Yes, darling, I'm hearing it again. Please call Ron quickly and let's get the hell over to where they are."

Jake quickly looked up Ron's number in his Contacts list and dialed him.

CHAPTER 18

Hardly anyone knew it, but Marie Komar had always had an ass fetish. It had been there right from when she was a little girl and had developed in leaps and bounds once she'd hit puberty.

She'd experimented sexually with herself for years and realized that while she could reach orgasm in the conventional way, she orgasmed best and in multiples when someone played with her anus.

This fact had so far been hard to communicate to Ron, who like most horny young men of his age, simply desired to stick his dick into her pussy and have his randy way with her.

Wham, bam, thank ya, ma'am.

And so, while their first few sexual encounters had been okay, Marie hadn't enjoyed herself as much as she knew she could.

She planned on rectifying that oversight tonight.

Seeing as Ron was already both stoned and horny, it took Marie a bit of explaining to communicate what she wanted to him. But finally, Ron agreed to lick her ass while she stroked herself to climax.

To accomplish this, Marie slipped off her panties and got down on her hands and knees.

"Okay, get behind me and start licking," she said in stoned tones, being only slightly less alcohol-and-narcotic-disorientated than her boyfriend. But yes, she still felt in control of the situation. She was having her ass licked tonight and that was that.

So, Ron got down behind her and began licking. And it was very good. In fact, it was extremely good. Ron had a nice thin tongue and Marie relaxed her sphincter so that his tongue could slip inside of her. Which she knew lots of guys didn't enjoy, but Ron and she had already reached the agreement that after she came this way, Ron could fuck her in the ass as compensation, which he was really looking forward to.

It took some practice to be able to rub oneself between the legs like this, it being necessary to balance oneself on only three limbs while doing so, but Marie had had over a decade of practice at such contortions, so no problem there.

The sensation, was fantastic, incredible. "Oh, Ron baby, I just love you so much," Marie gasped as his tongue roved back and forth and inside her relaxed anus. "Yeah, honey, just keep on like that! Yes, fucking like that!"

Marie knew she would orgasm at any moment now, and it would be one of the greatest climaxes she'd ever had.

But then the phone rang.

And Ron, that idiot, stopped licking her and picked it up to answer it. And as Marie listened to him talk on the phone, all of her delicious sensations drained out of her crotch, leaving her empty. Empty and extremely angry, an anger which only increased as she heard some of the things Ron said:

"Yeah? Hey, bro. How's it goin' . . . Oh, you've arrived? Oh, Tom's asleep. Dunno, but the guy was all tired out from work—had a hard week, you know how it is. Sara too, I think. . . . Oh, we'd all been drinking . . . lots of great booze. Where are you? . . . On the trail? Left trail or right? . . . No, no, you guys are definitely going the right way. Just keep walking that way. And once you hit the river, you gotta turn right and keep going too. Yeah, right, not left. . . . Five minutes tops. . . . Sorry, dude, gotta run. I was eating Marie's ass out when you called. . . . Yeah, I don't think she came yet before you called . . . she looks mad as fuck, and I ain't even fucked her yet. . . . Okay, see ya in five."

And with those misleading instructions passed on to his unfortunate friends, Ron Nicoles turned his attention back to his girlfriend. "So, alright, baby, where were we?"

But any suggestion that they were about to carry on where they'd left off were cut short when Marie screamed, "Get out!" at him.

"Come on, honey, simmer down," Ron said. "Just kneel down again and I'll resume licking you."

But Marie, who was now sitting down on their camping mattress with her legs crossed in front of her, had picked up her cellphone to throw at him.

She flung the cellphone at Ron. He ducked it and it missed him and hit the tent canvas and then the ground. But the danger was far from over, as Marie was already reaching for one of her boots. The boot was a heavy one, and in the time it took Marie to pick it up and properly aim it at him, Ron quickly slipped out of the tent.

"Get lost, you betraying sonofabitch!" Marie screamed after him. "Ron, if I see you again in this tent tonight, I'll cut your useless dick off."

She was quite loud. If she kept shouting, she might wake up both Tom and Sara, who wouldn't appreciate the disturbance.

But most important of all, Ron suddenly remembered that his gun was in the tent, and he also realized that Marie could still make out his silhouette through the tent walls, and in her incensed state she just might dig out his gun from their luggage and attempt to shoot his dick off.

And worst of all, he had a hard-on.

"Damn," he said, still too high to really worry about his situation. "The girl must be on the rag or something." He thought he heard Marie weeping in their tent as he stepped away from it, but the night had a lot of noises and his ears may have been deceiving him.

"And who the hell wants to eat a woman's ass anyway?" he said, once sure Marie couldn't hear him.

With that stated to no one in particular, Ron walked out of the campsite. He still had one of the joints they'd rolled earlier on him, and on discovering he was fortunate to also have a lighter with him, he lit up the marijuana cigarette and got down to smoking it.

On reaching the river, it occurred to Ron to go look for Jake and Nina, to ensure they hadn't gotten lost from the directions he'd given them. Simple directions for sure, but Ron knew that some people couldn't even visit the barbershop at the corner without getting lost.

"Nah, they'll be okay," Ron said, and instead turned and walked the other way towards the west bridge, where he sat down and got even higher than he already was.

CHAPTER 19

"Damn, the guy was stoned again," Jake told Nina after he hung up.

"What did he say?"

"That he was licking his girlfriend's asshole when I called, and she's not pleased about the interruption." Jake burst out laughing. "Can you imagine that?"

Despite her fears, Nina burst out laughing too. Then she calmed down a little and became serious again. "But what did he say about our location?"

Jake sighed. "According to Ron, we're heading in the right direction and should reach the river at any moment now." He reached out and took his wife's arm. "C'mon, sweetheart, let's keep going, we're almost there."

Nina shook her head. "Baby, I'm getting a real bad feeling about this. You just said the guy was stoned, so much so that he's revealing the details of his sex life. How the hell do we know that he gave us the right directions? If he's that stoned, he could send us to Spruce Knob Lake and think he was talking about the Shavers Fork river here by the camp."

Jake scratched his chin. "Hmm, you're making a lot of sense. But what do we do then? Head back to the car and pass the night in it and try to locate everyone in the morning when they've all sobered up again? I'd have suggested reading the directions in Tom's cellphone text again, but they'll be no use at all from our current posi—"

"Shush!" Nina said. "It's nearby!"

"Huh?" Jake was startled. Nina had suddenly frozen stiff, like a hound that smelled a rabbit nearby.

"The thing that's been following us is close by," Nina said. Then she shone her flashlight into the trees and Jake saw what she meant. The flashlight revealed a pair of strangely unnatural eyes, staring back at them both.

"Shit, what is that?" Jake asked, taking a step back when the creature, which had originally appeared to be just a raccoon, suddenly opened its mouth, revealing more teeth that any raccoon had a right to have. And it was drooling too, like a rabid animal.

"We need to move away from it," Nina said, but it was too late. The raccoon, which also seemed to have glowing orange eyes, suddenly burst into motion.

What happened next startled Jake. Moving like a blur of darkness, the raccoon leapt up onto Nina's shoulder and began biting away at her neck, while Nina began shrieking. Jake then grabbed hold of the raccoon and tried to pull it off of Nina, but the creature was holding on fast to her, all the while with its teeth chomping away at her throat. When pulling on the raccoon failed to get it off of Nina, Jake began hitting it with his flashlight. By now, Nina's blood was spraying everywhere, including over her husband, and a horrible gurgling sound had already entered into her shrieking.

And then, seemingly out of nowhere, Nina's head separated from her shoulders and fell off of her body. The raccoon was still standing on Nina's shoulders and before her headless corpse toppled down to the ground, it hissed at Jake and leapt at him.

But by then Jake was already running for his life.

He ran with terror in his heart and tears in his eyes. No, what just happened was impossible. A raccoon—a fucking raccoon of all things—hadn't just bitten off his wife's head. No, that was impossible. Even movies hadn't yet descended down to that level of absurdity, which would be similar to a cat or dog being able to bite its way through a person's neck in a matter of seconds.

It's eyes! Its fucking eyes were orange!

That detail also made no sense. How could a creature have orange eyes? He'd seen pictures of rabid raccoons once or twice, and their eyes didn't look like what he'd seen in the flashlight glare, in the moments before it had attacked; eyes all one solid color like they'd been painted over.

Was the animal rabid or what?

Once or twice Jake looked around, but he saw no sign of the raccoon, but that of course meant very little, a raccoon was a woodland creature, it couldn't be expected to run on a fixed trail like a human would. The damn thing was most likely lurking in the trees.

After a while Jake stopped running. He'd both run out of breath and also realized that he once more had no idea where he was. Yes, he taken off running towards the parking lot, but how far off was it now? He'd dropped his flashlight when the killer raccoon had leapt at him and so couldn't shine its beam into the distance for visual confirmation.

Have I gotten turned around or not? No, no, this is the right way! Shit, Nina's dead, killed by that damn thing! No, I don't believe that animal is rabid; something a lot worse is wrong with it! I need to call for help!

On remembering his cellphone, he patted himself down twice, searching his pockets for it. But the phone was gone too, also apparently a victim of the fight with the crazed raccoon.

For a moment, Jake considered going back for his cellphone. In all probability, the damn beast would have left now. But the chilling memory of Nina's head popping off her body like a champagne cork advised against the wisdom of such course of action.

No, the sensible thing to do is to reach the car and drive to town to report things. Thank goodness I still have the car keys. He began weeping again. *Shit that thing killed my Nina! Oh, God, no!*

Jake resumed running again. Managing to overcome his grief for a while, he'd just remembered his younger brother and his brother's friends, who were all still somewhere in these same woods.

And I don't have my cellphone to call anyone to alert them to the danger! Shit! I have to reach my car and drive into town fast. The cops and forest rangers have to get here fast. More loss of life must be prevented. I can do it! I can do it! For Nina's sake I must do it!

Jake finally spotted his car. Less than a hundred yards away now. Now he ran with relief mingled in with his grief. He pulled out his car keyfob and unlocked the car door. Then he similarly turned the engine on. The car lights came on, creating false twilight in that area of the parking lot.

So far Jake had seen no further sign of the murderous little beast. But now, Jake suddenly began hearing sounds on the trail behind him. Caught between the choices of seeing what was making the noises and dashing into the car, which was barely twenty yards away now, Jake chose the former. And then he once more found himself unable to believe his eyes.

What the fuck!?

His heart leapt up into his mouth on seeing that the deadly raccoon was finally coming after him. And was moving so fast that Jake realized he'd never reach the car door before it reached him. So instead, he leapt aside as the beast neared him. He hit the gravel floor of the parking lot and rolled over. Then, ignoring his bruises from his fall, he leapt to his feet and looked around.

At first, he didn't see the raccoon and he imagined he'd successfully evaded it.

Okay now, I can still make it out of here. I just gotta make it into the car and then I'm safely outa here.

But then Jake looked at his car and realized that the raccoon was lying on top of it.

No, the crazy beast wasn't lying down, it was crouching there, waiting for me to get up!

He realized this as the raccoon launched itself through the air at him and hit him in the chest.

Once more Jake Jackson was struck with total disbelief as the raccoon began digging its way through his body, tunneling though him with such violence that in less than a minute it had ripped its way out through his back and leapt down onto the sand again.

And by then Jake Jackson was dead, dead, dead.

Elvis next ran down to the river and bathed himself thoroughly, cleaning as much blood as he could off of himself.

Once that was done, the raccoon crossed the bridge and hurried to the spot beneath the cabin where he had left his stash of orange 'candy.'

Elvis was alarmed to find the Agent Orange all gone.

And then he began to have the junkie shakes.

CHAPTER 20

It was about midnight, when, unable to sleep, Charlotte Bentley walked out onto the front porch of she and Gary's cabin in the woods.

The evening had been a bittersweet one. Charlotte currently felt depressed because of she and Gary's argument earlier. Seated outside on the front porch with a shawl wrapped around her to keep out the cold, she felt saddened that they'd argued so heatedly. Gary was already fast asleep in their bed, but she'd been unable to fall asleep. So, she sat in her chair and stared out through the porch screen at the forest beyond, and wondered if maybe her husband was right and there was something wrong in a human being as close to wild animals as she was.

And it was then that she heard the wheezing noise. The noise was coming from the raccoon pet-flap at the far side of the porch screen. Something about the noise immediately bothered Charlotte. The creature out there sounded distressed. And why, if it was one that was familiar with her, didn't it push its way up onto the porch?

The creature out there might be dangerous.

But despite those worries, Charlotte hurried into the house to get a flashlight. Once she was thus equipped, she hurried outside the house again, and lifted up the pet door herself.

She was surprised to see Elvis crawl in through the pet door. The raccoon was shaking badly like a person with a fever, and when it looked up at her as if pleading for help, there seemed to be something wrong with its eyes, which had an unnatural orange glint to them.

Then Elvis flopped over like he was dying and lay wheezing and sputtering on the front porch.

With no idea what was going on with her little friend, Charlotte immediately panicked and ran inside to wake Gary up.

***

"So, what's wrong with the little thief now?" Gary Bentley asked on stepping outside. "Indigestion from eating too much lunchmeat?"

He was still angry with Charlotte and at first imagined she'd only woken him on a pretext to continue their argument about her feeding the animals.

But his indifference changed the moment he saw Elvis. He knelt down by the animal's side and made a cursory inspection of its body. Yes, Elvis was wet, like maybe he'd fallen into the river and maybe he'd caught a bad cold in the water. But that definitely didn't explain the orange color of Elvis's eyes, a color which seemed uncannily familiar to him, like he'd seen that same color recently, but his sleepy mind was delaying making the connection.

In fact, the longer Gary examined the wheezing and sputtering raccoon, the deeper a disturbing idea crept into his mind and refused to leave.

"You know, honey," he told Charlotte in a confused voice, "if I didn't know better, I'd think our little friend here was having withdrawal symptoms."

"It's that candy you brought home," Charlotte instantly replied. "I told you that stuff was drugs, not candy, but you didn't believe me."

"No way." But now Gary's mind made the connection: the wheezing raccoon's eyes were the same shade of orange as the 'candy.' "Only one way to be sure, honey," he told Charlotte. "Fetch the plastic bag with the candy, and let's see if he recognizes it."

Charlotte vanished through the entrance, and soon returned with the bag of little orange rocks.

"Okay, so now I'll just wave it at him and see if he recognizes it or not," Gary said. "If he does, no harm done. We'll keep an eye on him while he goes cold-turkey, and take him to the vet if he shows signs of getting worse."

The effect of waving the pack of 'candy' at Elvis was something neither Gary nor Charlotte had anticipated. From initially lying flat on his side as if dying and wheezing and sputtering in seeming abject misery, the raccoon was up on its feet again in seconds. It began making a barking noise, and showing its teeth to the couple, who were simultaneously struck by the thought that Elvis now had more teeth than before. And there was also the raccoon's glowing orange gaze to consider.

"Whoa, down, boy!" Gary said, lifting the bag of drugs well out of Elvis's reach, with the raccoon standing on its rear legs and pawing his pants legs trying to reach them. Gary was shocked by the raccoon's behavior. Elvis looked as desperate as a human junkie, like his life depended on his acquiring the orange rocks in the bag.

"And I thought selling drugs to kids in playgrounds was nasty," Charlotte quipped. "Who'd ever have imagined we'd wind up with crackhead wildlife too?"

Then she gasped. "Honey, watch out!"

Gary, who'd turned to laugh at what she'd just said, hadn't seen Elvis leap up from the floor with his jaws opened to bite.

However, Gary reacted just in time, flinging up his hand and brushing Elvis harmlessly aside, though this resulted in his dropping the packet of drugs too.

But before Gary could bend to retrieve the packet of drugs from the floor, Elvis had snapped it up in his jaws. A moment later, the raccoon had bolted, and Gary and his wife were both staring at the swinging pet door.

After a while, Gary sighed. "We're gonna have to get the li'l fella into rehab before he overdoses on that shit and kills himself."

Even Charlotte found that uproariously funny.

Gary extended a hand to her. "Come on, baby, let's go to bed. Nothing more we can do tonight. I'll have a look at Elvis's hiding place again in the morning. He ain't smart enough to think of somewhere else to hide his drugs."

Charlotte happily accepted Gary's proffered hand, and pressed close against him. And that was how their husband-wife spat ended.

CHAPTER 21

"So, babe, how you feelin' now?" Denny asked as he watched Tess suck in the pale crack fumes. "This shit holding you for the moment?"

Tess grinned and fell back against the ratty couch the cabin had to offer. She grinned at Denny with her eyes glazed over in stupor. "It's good, man," she said. "But you already promised me that the best is yet to come, didn't'cha?"

Denny nodded. "Yeah, I sure did. Tomorrow morning we'll have another look for the Agent Orange we lost and if we don't find it, I'll ring up Max for another batch of product."

"Is he gonna be upset you lost this batch?" Tess asked dreamily, sucking in more narcotic smoke and then falling back like she'd been hit with a sledgehammer.

Denny shook his head. "Nah. Max even told me we need to give away some free samples as marketing, you know enticement to lure in fresh customers."

He got up from where he'd been sitting on the couch and walked over to stare out the windows, trying to locate Tom and his friends' camp in the darkness. But even though the group's tents were arranged almost opposite this cabin, the intervening trees made them impossible to make out with the moon currently behind the mountain.

Denny studied the surface of the river for a while, then turned his attention back into the room, looking again at Tess. "I sure wish I could turn Tom and his friends on to our product," he said. "Those guys are loaded."

Tess laughed. "They won't be loaded for long if you make crackheads out of them all, and they know it. I could read the horror in their eyes when you offered them some free rock."

Denny laughed. "Yeah, yeah, but a drug dealer's gotta be optimistic. You know what I mean?"

"If you're referring to the way you're looking at my breasts, I got you covered, honey," Tess said, spreading her legs so he could see her white panties and the red pubic curls escaping their edges. "I promised to take care of you this weekend and I'm gonna keep my word. How do you want it tonight? A blowjob or do you wanna fuck?"

"A blowjob sounds just right," Denny said.

But Tess shook her head. "Nah, dude, get naked and let's fuck. It's been ages since I've been fucked properly."

Denny didn't believe that was true, but who was he to say no, when his penis suddenly felt so hard it might break off in his pants? So he took off his clothes, slipped a rubber on his erection, and got on top of Tess, who had also stripped naked in the interim and now spread her thighs wide to accommodate him.

"What I want you to do now," she purred in gentle tones, "is to fuck me really hard. That's what I'm in the mood for tonight. You've gotta really put your back into it." She yawned and spread her arms. "Can you do that, baby? Fuck me hard as a biker would?"

"You betcha!"

Tess did not move much as Denny pounded her. She laid back and let him do as he liked with her body, occasionally restating her requirement that he made love to her hard and fast.

After Denny had ejaculated and fallen asleep on her, Tess rolled him off of herself and onto the threadbare couch.

For a moment she laughed mockingly down at his naked slumbering figure, the condom full of semen slowly slipping off of his detumescent penis. The whole point of her insisting that Denny bang her hard was to get him so exhausted that he'd immediately pass out afterwards.

Once she was certain Denny Hallman would not be waking up for a good while, Tess dressed up and slipped out of the cabin's front door.

***

Tess laughed once more as she closed the cabin door on the sleeping drug dealer.

She wasn't exactly the airhead Denny thought she was. She had a secret, a secret that she had been hiding from Denny all day long.

Tess had already sampled Agent Orange and become addicted to it. She hadn't gotten her test sample from Denny, but from an old hobo named Micah, now resident in the county morgue, who had been one of the first unfortunates to overdose on Agent Orange.

Tess had been with Micah when he overdosed and had even been the one who'd called 911 to try and save him, but not before she had stashed the rest of the small orange rocks he'd been smoking into her handbag.

From there, it has been a short step to full addiction, with her only problem being where to get a constant supply of the wonderful orange stuff, without having to keep screwing Denny for it, which had initially been difficult to figure out, seeing as according to Micah, Denny was the only supplier in town.

But then had come the wonderful occurrence of Denny losing control of his car and attracting police attention and she having to cast his stash of Agent Orange into the nearby woods. There was a whole lot of Agent Orange in that lost package, enough to keep her high for a month. All Tess had to do now was find the drug before Denny did and she could get as high as the sky if she wanted to without have to suck Denny off for the privilege.

But despite the superlative high it provided, Agent Orange had its disadvantages also.

Foremost among these was the already stated fact that this orange crack variation killed some of its uses. Another side effect (and a visual clue to the drug's usage) was the way in which it turned some of its users' eyes a bright glowing orange color.

But I'm not one of those two categories, Tess thought with relief as she descended the front cabin steps. *My only problem is that taking Agent Orange makes me violent.*

This drug rage had already resulted in Tess killing two people, both of them homeless bums no one would ever miss and whom the police would most likely never find, because in a burst of the amazing strength that the drug had also given her, Tess had dug a deep grave in the basement of the abandoned old tenement the bums lived in and had buried their corpses there.

So, violence was one side effect of Agent Orange that affected Tess. The other one, in her case at least, as she hadn't met enough fellow addicts to compare notes, was a distressing (although also potentially useful ability) to smell the drug when it was nearby.

This ability was the reason why she had not initially followed Denny and his friends back to their car earlier in the day; though unable to locate the drug, she had been able to smell it. She had known it was nearby, almost near enough to reach out and touch if she had possessed x-ray vision and could see through the trees and bushes.

The scent of the orange rock was in her nostrils now, and, unlike earlier, when she had been with Denny and his friends, and as such had been unable to follow her nose to the end of the cocaine rainbow, she did not intend to lose the scent now.

Her first point of call was beneath the front porch, where she could smell a trace amount of the drug. Shining a flashlight beneath the cabin, Tess quickly located the source of the smell, a small nook filled with the remnants of a half-eaten lunchmeat packet. But the Agent Orange was now gone. However, it had clearly been there earlier, as evidenced by a barely visible smattering of drug powder inside the hole.

Where the hell is it now? That's the fucking million-dollar question. It's nearby, that's for sure. I can smell it nearby.

Already Tess's nerves had begun tingling in anticipation of reliving that superlative high.

She got up from her crouch beside the porch, and looked around in the darkness, attempting to locate the direction in which the scent of the drug was strongest.

Finally, it dawned on her just where the tantalizing smell was coming from.

Gotcha! she thought, smiling as her eyes settled on the other cabin at this part of the river bank, which stood just a hundred yards away. *So you just moved it over to the other cabin, did you?*

Very amused now, Tess set out for the cabin.

Two minutes later she had reached it and climbed the front porch steps. Here, the guiding scent was coming from inside the house, not from outside.

But who the hell found it and hid it in here I guess I'll never know, she thought as she pushed the cabin door open and stepped inside into the darkness.

Shining her flashlight around the cabin's front room, Tess was surprised to find the drug placed right out in the open on a similar ratty old couch to that on which Denny was currently sleeping. What really shocked her though, was the raccoon that was eating some of the orange 'candy.'

"Hey, that's mine, you can't have it," Tess said. Keeping the flashlight shining on the raccoon, she hurried over to the table and reached out to snatch up the plastic bag. "Didn't you hear me, you rat? I said scram! Get lost! That shit is mine! And I'm not sharing it with you!"

She had expected this tirade to scare the raccoon off. Only the little beast didn't budge, instead it lifted his head and hissed at her.

Tess was startled on seeing its orange eyes, eyes which in the glare of her flashlight give the impression of being twin balls of fire. *Fuck! This little beast is dangerous. This little shithead is an addict too, just like me.*

Still the craving was on her now. Tess did not intend to be denied her fix. Once more she reached out to grab the plastic bag.

And then the damn raccoon bit her.

"What the fuck?" Tess screamed, instantly jerking her hand back and examining the wound.

What she saw infuriated her, a semicircle of deep teeth marks on the back of her hand from which blood oozed. Turning her hand over revealed a similar bleeding semicircle on her palm.

"Oh, so ya wanna play it the hard way, do ya?" she screamed at the raccoon, suddenly out of her mind with both pain and anger, anger that only increased when the animal made no attempt to depart from the precious stash of agent orange, but instead hunched over it in a protective gesture, both continuing to bare its teeth at Tess and hissing at her.

The two addicts, human and animal, stared each other down, neither willing to give ground. And then, after positioning her flashlight on a side table in such a way that it flung its beam directly onto the couch, Tess snatched up a loose two-by-four from the floor and swung it at the greedy raccoon.

Whack! Suddenly the raccoon was airborne, zipping across the cabin's front room like a baseball heading for a home run. But then it hit the wall on Tess's left and bounced back at her. It landed on her left shoulder and attempted to sink its teeth into her neck. Tess easily brushed it off, and when it leapt at her again, once more with its fangs bared to bite, she whacked it again with her improvised baseball bat, which she now realized had nails sticking out of the end she'd been hitting the raccoon with, though the nails appeared not to be doing any lasting damage to the creature. Apparently, both times she'd hit the raccoon with the two-by-four, the nails had been facing the wrong direction.

But still, it looked like she'd hurt it this second time around. At least she'd slowed it down a little. It lay in a far corner with blood dripping from its left shoulder, a sight that gave Tess a sense of satisfaction.

"Yeah, asshole, that serves you right," she told it. "Okay, listen up. You want the crack and I want the crack. Fair enough, so we're going to share it. But as I'm obviously bigger than you and need more of the drug, I'll take most of it and I'll leave you one or two rocks that should keep you high for a while."

The raccoon hissed suspiciously at her and she thought she had gotten a message through to it. Indeed, it made no move towards or even as she bent over the couch to retrieve the package.

But then some crackhead sixth sense seemed to kick in in Tess's crazed and addled mind.

This is too easy, she thought. *If it was me, I wouldn't give up the drug this easily.*

That realization saved her life. She spun around and then instantly ducked out of the raccoon's way, as it sailed through the air at her, its teeth clamping tight towards her throat as it went past.

By now Tess felt really pissed off. "Fine, so you won't share. Your loss. I'll take it all for myself then."

That decided, she threw caution to the wind, dropped her improvised club on the table with the flashlight, and snatched up the plastic packet. To her amazement, the raccoon grabbed the other end of the plastic packet and refused to let go of it. And all of Tess's drug-fueled desperate strength could not tear the package of Agent Orange away from that little animal.

She felt she was going crazy. *How the hell did you get this strong, you little freak? Have you been working out or what?*

"Let go, let go, fucking let go of it!" she screamed in a rising crescendo, while the raccoon hissed at her just as loudly, its orange eyes projecting a desperation equal to hers.

Tess tugged and yanked, but so did the raccoon. It was a total stalemate.

As if it had been working out too, the plastic bag containing their drug of contention also stretched a little but refused to tear, which to Tess's mind was actually a relief as it meant she wouldn't later have to search the cabin floor for scattered orange chunks.

"Fucking let go of it!" she shrieked madly, as they each pulled on an end of the package.

But the raccoon just hissed back at her and bared its teeth some more.

And that was how Denny and Ron found the pair of them when they entered the cabin to investigate the noise.

CHAPTER 22

Once awakened by the strange noises coming from downriver, it had taken Denny Hallman a few minutes to pull his clothes on before he could leave the cabin.

While dressing, he'd quickly identified the screaming voice as Tess's, and had become very scared for her safety, fearing that a serial killer had somehow lured her down to the nearby cabin and was butchering her there.

Once dressed, Denny grabbed up a flashlight and a knife and ran out of the cabin, and then ran towards the other wooden building.

At the bridge he ran into Ron, who was also heading towards the far cabin to investigate the noise.

"What the fuck is going on in there?" Ron asked as they ran on together.

"Fuck if I know," Denny replied. "All I can hear is the same as you can. She keeps telling someone to let go of something. But who, and what?"

Tess's screaming was currently settled at a regular volume of anger. In between her speaking, they could also hear loud hissing and growling.

Ron and Denny reached the cabin, charged up its steps at breakneck speed, and flung the door open.

"Hey, asshole, stop whatever the fuck it is that you're doing to her!" Denny growled protectively, before stopping and gaping in amazement at the crazy scene before them.

"Dude, is that a fucking raccoon?" Ron enquired in an equally shocked voice.

No matter how hard they tried to, neither young man could immediately work out why Tess and a raccoon (of all creatures) were involved in a tug-of-war over what Denny immediately recognized as his missing package of Agent Orange.

CHAPTER 23

"Give it to me! It's mine, you little creep!" But then Tess realized that she and her animal companion weren't alone in the cabin anymore.

What happened next was borderline telepathic. Tess and the raccoon glanced knowingly at each other and an unspoken communication flashed between them, the coded knowledge that these two people who had just entered the cabin were enemies of theirs, nonbelievers who would take their precious stash of Agent Orange away from them for ever and ever. This deadly enemy needed to be attacked and defeated and their threat laid to rest for good.

And if either Tess or the raccoon had had the slightest doubt about the dire seriousness of their shared crisis, this doubt was completely erased when Denny stepped towards them.

"Hey, baby, where did you find the Agent Orange?" was all Denny managed to say before Tess screamed, "Git im, boy!" at the raccoon, snatched up her spiked two-by-four from the table, and swung it at Denny's head.

CHAPTER 24

Denny saw the club coming towards his head too late to do anything about it. The two-by-four hit him and knocked him back towards the wall, where he stood stunned and panting, not yet realizing that he'd escaped death only because, in her haste to kill him, Tess had not properly aligned the club so that its spikes were aimed at his head.

But beside him, Ron hadn't been as lucky. Denny was now treated to the absurd and horrifying sight of watching a raccoon eat its way down into a living human being's head, chewing through the skull bone like it was mere cardboard. At first Ron tried to pull the vicious creature off, but his efforts were completely ineffectual and soon ceased, after which he slumped down to the floor, with the crazy orange-eyed raccoon still clinging at him and biting into his head and spitting out chunks of his brain matter, while Ron's squirting blood painted it a ghastly red.

Denny had seen enough. Saved from a follow-up attack by Tess simply because she had also been engrossed in watching the deadly raccoon's destruction of Ron, Denny now realized that his own life was in grave danger.

This point was brought home very clearly to him by Tess, who swung her club at him again, this time with its spiking of nails properly aimed at his face.

But this time Denny had seen it coming. He ducked under her swing, leapt back, and made it safely out through the front door before Tess could unstick the two-by-four from the cabin wall and attack him again. Also, Denny wanted to be far away before that crazy raccoon turned its murderous attentions to him also.

Shit, he thought as he dashed down the steps, *I gotta get across the river and warn the others that Tess has gone crazy. And that killer coon! What the fuck is going on with that thing? I ain't never seen—Oh, shit!*

Denny had been dashing down the front steps without looking, and in the dark he tripped and went sprawling.

And now when he had escaped the initial danger, Denny's run of good luck had finally run out.

The short fall to the ground broke Denny's neck, twisting his head violently on his shoulders.

In the few seconds of life left to him before he died, Denny Hallman cursed the day that Max the chemist had introduced him to the variant of crack cocaine named Agent Orange.

CHAPTER 25

"Shit, he got away!" Tess thought, but then, peeking out through the cabin door and shining her light down its front steps, she saw that she was mistaken. Denny was lying flat on the floor at the bottom of the steps. And she didn't even need to go down there and kill him, gravity has done the job for her.

Denny clearly would not ever be getting up again; his neck was twisted one-eighty degrees on his shoulders, so that while he was lying flat on his belly, his face was looking up at her.

"Sorry, dude," she hissed down at him. "I guess tonight simply ain't your lucky night."

She shut the cabin door and turned back into the room, her eyes flickering with disinterest over Ron's ravaged remains.

"Okay, little guy," she told the raccoon. "Let's stop fighting. I have already pointed out you that there's enough crack in that bag for both of—"

Tess stopped talking, and just gaped at the couch in shock. The raccoon was gone, and no, it hadn't left the cabin alone. The sneaky little thief had taken the bag of crack along with it. It had left with the entire store of drugs. It has not left even one little rock for Tess to get high on.

"Damn that greedy little fucker," Tess spat. "Listen you little son of a bitch," she said calmly as if the raccoon was still there in the room with her, or was somewhere close by where it could still hear her. "You may not know this, but I can smell that crack you're carrying, and that means it doesn't matter how long it takes me to locate you, I will find you, and when I do, I will take all the crack for myself just like you just did, and then, you'll have nothing to get high on either. How does that sound for turnaround being fair play, you little piece of animal poop?"

Feeling crazy and realizing that she needed to get hold some of that precious Agent Orange before the crazy really took her over, Tess left the cabin. She made quite sure to bring her handy two-by-four along with her just in case she ran into the thieving raccoon again.

Another problem with Agent Orange was that, for Tess at least, once she'd tasted the orange stuff, regular crack cocaine held no more appeal for her. There was a whole baggie of regular crack in her purse, more than she could smoke in a week, and yet she felt no desire to load up her crack pipe and hit herself up with it. All she wanted was her Agent Orange, and the more Tess thought about the raccoon making off with the drug, the more crazed she grew; the more enraged she got.

"Damn that little fucker," she growled as she stepped over Denny's corpse. It occurred to her to hide the body, and so she dragged it away, and rolled it out of sight beneath the cabin's front porch.

With that little detail attended to, Tess hurried away, walking past she and Denny's erstwhile cabin, and heading towards the cabins at the farther bridge, over near the east trail. Just like a shark catching a scent of blood in distant water, she could smell Agent Orange over in that direction. That had to be where the raccoon was headed.

She needed to find that damn raccoon before it ate up all of the precious crack.

CHAPTER 26

It was morning again after a seemingly short night. With most of the forest creatures now back in bed, the Sleepaway Campground was quiet.

Inside one of the pair of tents near the river, Marie Komar was just waking up when she became aware of a strange sensation. At first, she felt a little alarmed, but then she understood what was happening.

Someone was licking her buttocks. The sensation was light, but rapid and feathery.

Marie relaxed. *Oh, Ron finally came back to make it up to me!*

Seeing as she wasn't fully awake yet and thus wasn't in any condition to get up on her hands and knees, Marie simply spread her legs wider to permit Ron better access to her anus. She didn't look around, as she thought doing so would spoil the thrill Ron was trying to give her. And besides, looking at him might break the spell, by reminding her of how he'd spoilt things last night.

So, Marie just made herself comfortable on the mattress and parted her legs very wide. Then she pulled the blanket tight around her head, and giggling to herself, relaxed to enjoy the experience.

It was very enjoyable. She felt Ron's fingers probing her, pushing her buttocks apart, and then very tentatively, starting to lick her rear entrance.

Flick, flick, the tongue went, licking away and probing inside her. Soon it was all Marie could do to keep from squirming.

Oh, it's so goddam hard to pretend to asleep now! Oh, Ron darling, just keep licking me like that! Yes, exactly like that! Hey, Ron doesn't have a beard, why the hell does he feel so hairy this morning?

Marie overlooked this incongruity for the time being,

The licking continued, until Marie knew she was going to orgasm soon without even fingering herself, a feeling that intensified when she felt Ron inserting himself into her anus. The insertion went slowly as if Ron was scared of the hole.

Yes, pleasure, more pleasure, and then a sudden discomfort, which was when Marie first realized that something was wrong between the cheeks of her ass.

"Hey, baby, go slower, you're starting to hurt me," she said. "Hey, take it easy!"

This last comment was made with lots of irritation, because now Marie was really being stretched, her asshole really starting to hurt.

"Hey, baby, stop hurting me!" And then Marie flung away the blanket and looked down at her crotch. To do so she had to roll over on her back.

And what she saw made her wonder how she could ever have been so dumb as to think Ron had been the one tending lovingly to her anus.

Something was moving between the cheeks of her ass, and now seemed to have forced its head all the way inside of her anus. Marie couldn't see it too clearly in the tent's interior shadows, but it looked and felt very hairy, and had arms and legs, so it clearly wasn't a snake.

A huge panic settled over her. Rising quickly to a sitting position, she grabbed hold of the animal and tried to get it out or her body. She was too confused by the crazy turn of events to scream.

And the animal, whatever it was, was continuing to force its way up into her body. She imagined she could even feel it licking around inside of her.

Oh, my God! Oh, my God, it's gonna rip me apart if I don't get it out of my butt!

Still she didn't scream, even though she'd now realized the danger to herself if the animal could get all of the way inside her. Marie didn't scream because she was worried about what her friends would think, if they found her like this, with—*Oh God, it's a raccoon, it's a damn raccoon, I'm being anally raped by a fucking raccoon!*

As Tess grabbed hold of the raccoon and attempted to pull it out of her body, her mind filled with the horrible social consequences for herself, should the others find her in her current straits. She'd never be able to live the rumors down.

I'll be famous on Facebook and YouTube. I'll in the same class as fucking Richard Gere and that damned gerbil! Oh no, you don't! Get the fuck out of my ass, you damn coon!

She'd have burst into tears if her situation wasn't so desperate. The last thing she needed at the moment was for Ron to walk in here. *I'll kill him if his timing is that bad.*

I've gotta get this critter out of my rectum, she thought, while tugging on it with all her might! "Get the hell out of me, you!"

Now that Marie was in a pragmatic state of mind, she felt that freeing herself from the raccoon shouldn't prove to be too difficult, as most of it was still outside of her.

But getting free of the animal was easier said than done.

Oh no! she thought as her anus stretched wider than it ever had before and the raccoon's shoulders vanished into her body.

Realizing that if its shoulders could slip into her body so easily, the rest of it was certain to follow just as easily, Marie altered her grip on the creature, letting go of its hairy flanks and taking a firm hold of it rear legs instead. A leg in each hand, she tugged as hard as she could. This too, was when she first noticed the little package of orange candies at the foot of the mattress.

Hey, that looks like the special crack Denny said he lost yesterday! But what's it doing here in my tent?

Her distraction cost her dearly. By the time she'd gotten her mind back on her impossible situation, the raccoon had forced its front legs up inside her ass too. Now, half of its body was inside of her and half was outside of her.

Oh no, you don't! she groaned mentally, resuming her struggle to prevent the thing from completely invading her. By now, she really wished she could yell for help, the feeling of something alien in her rectum felt like she had really bad constipation.

But the guys are gonna think I stuck this raccoon up my butt intentionally. I'll never live the shame down.

She made a final valiant attempt to pull the raccoon out. But it squirmed inside of her in such an uncomfortable way that she let go of its legs.

It bit me! It bit me inside my butt!

Before she could grab it again, the raccoon's hindquarters kicked violently and a few moments later, the entire creature had vanished inside of Marie's body, only its tail now dangled from her anus. Marie looked like she'd suddenly grown a two-toned tail.

Now her belly bulged like she was expecting a baby.

Fuck, I can't believe it! There's an animal in my butt! Okay, the good thing is that it's completely inside me. I'm still not gonna tell the guys about this. Oh, hell no! What the hell am I gonna do about this? Okay, I know how I'll handle it. I need to remain calm and collected like there isn't anything wrong with me. What I'll do is, I'll tell Tom and Ron that I've got bad women sickness and ask them to drive me to the ER—I'll be famous there after this but—

Then she felt a sudden pain inside of her body. *Shit! It's biting me again! No, no, stop it! Damn you, stop fucking biting me you little shithead!*

Marie grabbed hold of her swollen belly and began rolling around on the floor of the tent. She was trying her best not to scream, to hold in the pain and protect her good reputation, but it was becoming impossible, as the raccoon was biting her violently now. She felt a sudden warm flow between her buttocks and thought she'd shit herself. However, when she looked down, she sat that what she'd ejected was blood; not mud-colored excrement, but bright red blood that didn't stop flowing.

And the tearing pain inside of her didn't stop. It felt to her as if the raccoon was tunneling up through her from her belly to her chest. In addition to the blood squirting out between her legs, she could see the imprints of the raccoon's limbs outlined on her belly as it seemingly traveled up inside her.

As blood now spilled out between her lips, Marie Komar had a sudden sense that she was dying.

No longer caring what her friends nearby, or those on social media, would think about her, Marie began screaming now.

CHAPTER 27

Tom and Sara had both been fast asleep in the tent next to Marie's, but her screaming soon woke them up.

"What the hell is that?" Tom said, gripping his head to nurse his starting hangover.

"Baby, I think it's Marie. Something's wrong with her."

Tom forgot his headache and leapt up to his feet. "It sounds like Ron is beating the crap out of her," he said, pulling a tee shirt on over his shorts and then looking around for his flip-flops.

"Closely followed by Sara, Tom unzipped the tent flap and ran over to Ron and Marie's tent.

In the meantime, Marie's screams of pain had reached a crescendo, but then suddenly stopped.

"Hey, you guys, what's happening in there?" Tom asked cautiously from the tent opening. But there was no reply. In a way the silence from inside Ron and Marie's tent was even more frightening that the racket had been.

Fearing the worst, Tom pulled aside the tent flap and peeked in, with Sara leaning over his shoulder to see as well.

"What the hell happened in here?" Sara asked in fright.

To both their surprises, Ron wasn't in the tent. Marie was, but she was lying on her back on the floor, naked and with blood both on her face and her thighs. There was a lot of blood on the floor of the tent, but that wasn't the worst of it.

The worst thing was that something was moving *inside* Marie's body. The thing's motion was unmistakable—squirm, squirm, like she'd swallowed a huge snake.

Sara gripped Tom tight and together they stepped fully into the tent.

Marie was obviously dead. She had to be; nothing could have survived the way the thing inside her was churning up her chest cavity.

"What the hell is inside her?" Sara asked in a scared voice.

"I think we're about to find out," Tom replied, because right at that moment, Marie's throat started bulging.

"I think it's planning on coming out," Sara said, ducking behind Tom again as Marie's neck got fatter and fatter, until it was almost as thick as one of her thighs.

Then there was the loud snap of her jaws dislocating.

And then something began to emerge from her mouth.

The emerging creature took its time with getting out of its victim, and long before it was fully free of her, Tom and Sara had both recognized what it was, clearly identifiable by the black mask of its little gray face.

"That's a raccoon!" Tom gasped.

"Yeah, but . . . what . . . I mean, w-w-wh . . . ?" Sara added to his confused statement. "Why the hell did it attack Marie and fuck her up like this? Di-di-did she eat its nuts or what?"

And Marie really had been fucked up; in leaving her body through her face, the raccoon had completely distended her lower jaw, so that her chin was now almost level with her breasts.

"Shit, *Alien* has nothing on this!" Tom said in shock.

Now that it was fully emerged from Marie's head, the killer raccoon seemed to be considering its options. It sat on Marie's belly, staring at the two intruders and occasionally looking over at a plastic pack of candy that lay on the bedding. As was to be expected of a creature that had just burst out of a fresh corpse, the animal was completely covered in blood. But the scariest thing about it was its bright orange eyes, eyes that were all that single orange color. It stared from Tom and Sara to the bag of orange candy and back at them again. Finally, it leapt off of Marie and crouched over the candy, picked out a small candy chunk and began eating it.

"What do we do?" Sara asked, as they watched the raccoon.

"We need to call the cops," Tom replied her. "But first of all, we need to take pictures." He stepped back towards the tent flap, and pulled Sara along with him. "Come with me. I need to get my phone from our tent."

But Sara refused to move. She looked at Tom in disgust. "Pictures? Ugh, baby, how can you even think of a thing like that a time like this? Our friend is dead here and you're thinking of YouTube likes?"

"No, no," Tom quickly replied. "But if we don't snap this as evidence, no one's gonna believe us when we say a raccoon killed Marie."

"Oh, yeah, you're right," Sara agreed, her gaze once more riveted on the killer animal, which had now finished consuming its first orange candy and was now stuffing another one into its mouth. "Baby, why the hell are its eyes that weird orange color?"

"No idea, and I don't think either of us really wanna know the reason." He grabbed Sara by both of her shoulders. "Listen, are you coming with me to our tent to fetch my phone or not? Though maybe you wait here and keep an eye on the thing."

Sara immediately shook her head at his suggestion. "Hell no. I ain't remaining here with that evil thing. You wait, I'll go fetch your phone."

At the moment, the raccoon seemed to be unaware of them. It chewed its orange candy and the sound of its crunching was loud in the little tent.

You know, that orange candy is the same color as its eyes, Sara suddenly realized and next a shudder ran through her as she realized that while eating the orange candy, the raccoon seemed to be growing more and more agitated, like someone getting the shakes from an overdose of caffeine. At the moment the raccoon seemed to be sitting still by sheer willpower, as if its body wanted to run wild, but its appetite was holding it in check.

Yeah, Tom can have that thing. I wanna get far away from it. It looks like it's priming itself to attack someone; like that orange candy is some kinda energy source that it feeds off.

Sara turned to step out of the tent and go fetch their cellphones to record the evidence, but now Tom restrained her with a hand on her shoulder.

"Hold on, I've a better idea," he said. "I just remembered Ron's gun is in here somewhere. I'll get it out. That way, whoever remains behind will have some protection from the crazy critter."

"Yeah, so long as it's you who's staying here alone with it. . . . Hey, where's Ron anyway?"

"No idea. I hope our little friend here didn't kill him too." Tom was already bending down and rooting through Ron's luggage. "I'll call Ron once we get our phones. . . . Okay, so here we are," he added, pulling Ron's handgun out of his bag and holding it up to the light.

Unfortunately, that was the same moment at which the raccoon across the room seemed to have had enough candy. With a hiss and a bark, the animal launched itself across the room at Tom.

Afterwards, Sara realized that the animal's decision of whom to first attack had been made for it by sheer instinct. Tom was crouching down over Ron's baggage, and that apparently made the mad creature consider him a 'smaller' target, and herself a 'larger' one, because she was standing on her feet.

And the raccoon had taken the path of perceived least resistance.

"Watch out!" Sara screamed.

Tom almost got his hand up in time, but then the airborne raccoon landed on his face and began biting and clawing at it.

Tom howled and succeeded in knocking the raging animal away, but the damage had already been done. When he staggered towards Sara again, she saw that he was blind, both of his eyes rendered into bloody pits by the raccoon's teeth and claws.

A bloodcurdling scream now forming in her own throat, Sara hurried forward and grabbed Tom's hand. She pulled him towards her, then ducked behind him and shoved him towards the tent flap.

"Just keep going," she said. "I wanna pick up the gun!"

The raccoon was crouched near the gun, its bloodstained tail up on Marie's deformed face. At the moment Marie's presence in the tent was an afterthought. Her young life over, she was of no further consequence to proceedings until the current violent happenings in the tent had all been resolved.

Sara held a hand up to her own face to prevent herself from sharing the same fate as Tom, but she was able to retrieve the gun without being attacked. In fact, as she bent down and picked the weapon up, she was surprised to see the animal looking around as if suddenly it had gotten confused. Then it dashed across the room to its bag of candy and huddled protectively over it.

Sara had seen enough. She considered shooting the horrible beast, but after considering what might happen to her if she failed to hit and kill it on her first attempt to do so, she decided to go tend to her wounded boyfriend instead.

She stepped outside of the tent, and instantly screamed, "Watch out, baby!" at Tom again, the second time in less than five minutes.

Denny's girlfriend Tess was swinging a nail-studded two-by-four at Tom's head. Tom didn't escape this attack either. Unable to see what was happening, his attempt to turn towards Sara on hearing her warning cry merely resulted in him placing himself in a perfect position for Tess's wooden club to sink its spikes deep into the side of his head.

Sara watched what was happening to her boyfriend in disbelief.

His head cracked open and bleeding, Tom jerked in place for a moment, while Tess yanked the two-by-four out of head and struck him again with it. This time the nails ripped off a wide chunk of Tom's skull and also dug out a part of his brain.

That was it for Tom Jackson. He keeled over forward, and collapsed dead to the forest floor.

Sara now found her voice. "What the hell have you just done, you crazy slut!?" she screamed at Tess. "You just killed Tom!"

Tess leaned on the two-by-four like nothing out of the ordinary had just happened. "Where's that fucking raccoon?" she asked. "Don't lie to me that it isn't here. I can smell the rock it's got with it."

Still looking at Tess like she was mad, Sara pointed into the tent. "It's in there. Careful, it's dangerous."

Tess laughed. "Yeah? So am I."

Sara watched Tess walk into the tent, and then she ran over to kneel by Tom's side. She had been harboring a faint hope that her boyfriend might have survived Tess's crazy attack, but that hope was quickly dashed. Tom was obviously stone dead, as dead as Marie in the tent.

Anger filled Sara, along with confusion. She had no idea what was going on, nor why Tess had attacked Tom. She was in the mood for answers now, and she intended on getting some.

She got to her feet and looked toward the entrance to Ron and Marie's tent.

Tess was just emerging from the tent. The redhead had a look of incredible frustration on her face and her green eyes were blazing almost as fiercely as the killer raccoon's had been.

"The damn raccoon is fucking gone!" she shrieked at Sara in a voice that screamed of madness. "It was here and now it's gone!"

"Yeah," Sara agreed in a tired voice, while wondering why she was even discussing this. "The fucking raccoon was here, and it killed Marie, just like you killed Tom. What's this about anyway?"

"That little thief has my special crack cocaine," Tess said. Then, as if soliloquizing, she yelled aloud, seemingly to no one in particular: "Oh, you can't run and hide from me, you hairy little thief," Tess shouted. "I can smell that precious rock you've got on you. Wherever you are, I can sniff it out. I know you're around here somewhere and I'm gonna find you. I'm definitely gonna find you."

After she was through with her tirade, Sara asked. "What special crack are you ranting about?"

Tess flung her a mean look. "The same orange shit we were searching for by the road yesterday. It was Denny's stash, but now that he's dead, it's all mine. And I'm gonna get it back."

"Wait a minute," Sara said. "Did you just say that Denny is dead?"

Tess nodded and gestured back out of the clearing, towards the nearby river. "Yeah, he and Ron both had accidents in one of the cabins last night."

Sara lifted her eyebrows. "Accidents?"

Tess made a face. "Look, the raccoon and I killed both of them, okay? Well, no, Denny's death actually *was* an accident, that happened when I was trying to kill him. But now that I've killed Tom, everyone's gonna assume I pushed Denny to his death anyway." Then her scowl deepened. "And now, I gotta kill you too, bitch, so you can't tell the cops anything about any of this." She pointed her two-by-four at Ron and Marie's tent. "The raccoon's escaping from me is all you and Tom's fucking fault anyway. You're the ones that scared it off, or else I've have gotten my drugs back from it by now."

With the two-by-four now threateningly raised, Tess stepped menacingly towards Sara.

Sara didn't hesitate. She waited until Tess was close enough so she wouldn't miss hitting her, and then she raised the gun in her hand and shot Tess in the face.

Tess looked confused for a second before Sara's second shot blew her head apart. And then she collapsed dead right on top of Tom's corpse.

In an angry daze, Sara stood over Tess's corpse and kept firing into her body until the revolver clicked empty.

Then, with the firearm dangling at her side, she turned her mind back to her problems.

So far as I can tell, there are now five corpses around here. Where the hell is that killer raccoon anyway? What I need to do now is get my phone from the tent and call the cops!

That settled in her mind, she began walking back to the tent she and Tom had shared. Then she stopped in her tracks when the killer raccoon popped its murdering little head out of the tent she was heading for.

Sara sighed. She had no intention of going close to the creature, not after what she'd watched it do to Marie. *And that bitch Tess just said it also killed Ron.*

Sara was suddenly aware of how alone she was out here, with apparently no other campers having yet arrived for the weekend. She was scared shitless of the animal across from her, and yet she would have to face it alone if it attacked.

Meanwhile, the raccoon was still watching her with its shiny orange eyes, while feeding its orange 'candy' into its bloody little mouth.

Sara looked down at the gun she was holding, realizing that in her hatred of Tess, she'd wasted her sole mode of defense.

Dammit! But I can reload—Ron has a pack of spare bullets in the trunk of his car. Okay, I need to rethink my strategy. I don't like the way that little monster is looking at me. Oh, so was it actually hiding from Tess just now? Could she really smell it out? Now, this is what I'm gonna do: I can't enter our own tent because the raccoon is in there, but I can still get into Ron and Marie's tent . . . I just need to slip inside there while it isn't looking my way. Shit! Why does it keep watching me? In their tent I can get both the keys to Ron's ride and also a cellphone I can at least make an emergency call on.

It seemed like a good plan and might have worked.

But once Sara stepped past Tom and Tess's corpses and started for the nearby tent, the raccoon suddenly burst into motion. It came charging at Sara.

With no way to defend herself now, Sara did the only wise thing. She flung her gun away and fled into the forest before the killer raccoon reached her.

CHAPTER 28

Forest ranger Gary Bentley was on the road early today. This was largely because his wife Charlotte had pushed him out of the house before breakfast and told him to go retrieve Elvis's package of weird crack before the raccoon overdosed on it.

"Yeah, she's right," Gary admitted aloud as he swung the ranger pickup truck onto the road leading to the Sleepaway campground. "Putting Elvis in rehab seemed like a good joke to make last night. Not so much this morning though. Hey, hey, what's this?"

Gary had just caught sight of a young woman running down the road towards him. As she got nearer to the truck, he could see that she was breathless, and had a look on her face of sheer panic.

Gary immediately parked the car and leapt down.

"Oh, thank God, thank God, you're here," the girl panted, running towards him.

"Hey, hey, miss, what's the matter?" he asked, catching her as she practically slammed her body into his and held him tightly, until he gently pulled away from her and looked into her eyes. From their brief contact he could feel her heart beating fast.

Her eyes were clear and she showed no sign of drug misuse, something that young campers were notorious for. Meaning that she really had been frightened out of her wits.

"What happened to you?" he asked in a gentle but authoritative voice.

It took the girl a little while to catch her breath. Then she gasped, "Killer raccoon, killer raccoon! It attacked me and my friends." She pointed behind her. "Fucking killer raccoon!"

Oh shit! This was Gary's sole thought on hearing her. It just had to be Elvis.

"Get in the truck," he told the girl. "Let's go back and check this out."

***

The first thing Gary noticed on arriving at the parking lot, was the large bloodstain on the ground, congealed in a mess of scraps of cloth and flesh on the parking lot gravel; and the red trail that led from it into the forest.

This all clearly looked like evidence of a crime, but Gary had no time to study it properly, because once he got down from the pickup truck, Sara, his young passenger, immediately grabbed his hand and began pulling him away towards the woods.

Drawing his gun from its holster in readiness for danger, Gary followed the young woman through the trees to she and her friends' camping site.

What he found on arriving there was a lot worse than he'd imagined. He stood at the edge of the clearing staring at two bodies, a female one lying on a male one, and winced at the damaged state of both corpses' heads.

"Fuck! Elvis did all this damage?" he exclaimed.

Sara, who'd now recovered herself a bit, looked at him strangely. "Wait, you just called it Elvis. You actually know the raccoon that did this?" she asked.

Gary lowered his gun to his side and sighed deeply. "I admit we're somewhat acquainted. My wife considers Elvis to be her pet."

"Hey, wait," Sara went on as they stepped closer to the bodies. "How can you be so sure it's the same raccoon? Has it attacked people before?"

Gary shook his head. "Not before last night anyway when it tried to bite me 'cos I'd taken away some kind of drug it had found."

Sara laughed coldly. "Alright, let me guess: the drug was some kinda orange 'candy' in a plastic bag?"

Gary looked at her sharply, then realized what her words meant. So, Elvis *was* the one that had killed these people. But no, that wasn't quite right.

"Okay, miss, I need some proper info now," he told Sara. He pointed down at the two corpses. As far as I can see, this lady beside us died of gunshot wounds. So, who shot her? And where's the girl you said Elvis killed?"

He listened while Sara explained in detail what had happened here at their campsite. Shit, once again, it was worse than what he'd expected. And once she was finished with her tale and he got up and walked into the tent where she said her friend was . . . well, Gary didn't think he'd be keeping any food down for the next week.

The dead young woman's completely dislodged jaw made it seem like she had on a slasher mask. And also, her body seemed unnaturally flat, like someone had ridden their car over it.

Maybe now my damn wife will believe me when I'm insisting it's bad to feed the wildlife!

Thankfully, Gary didn't find Elvis in there. He saw no other option than to kill the raccoon now, and yet wasn't looking forward to doing so. He still had fond memories of the little fellow.

He stepped out of the tent, back into the daylight. First things first. After waving to Sara to keep clear, and with his gun still held at the ready, Gary then hurried over to the second tent and peeked into that one too. Thankfully there were no additional corpses in there; but also, no Elvis either.

"So, what are you gonna do now?" Sara asked, when he walked back over to her, with his eyes scanning the surrounding tree trunks and his mind trying to figure out where his killer raccoon friend might be hiding now.

"First thing is to call in the regular police to deal with the bodies, including the two you mentioned that are hidden across the river." Gary frowned, then waved his pistol at her. "Then, while waiting for them to arrive, I'm gonna hunt down that little raccoon, before he can kill anyone else."

"No need to hunt it," Sara said. "It's been right here all along."

Gary didn't understand what she meant, but she pointed down at the two nearby corpses. Gary was treated to the strange sight of Elvis, bag of orange crack clenched tightly between his teeth, forcing his way out of the dead woman Tess's anus. The anus stretched and stretched like it would rip open, but it didn't and Elvis appeared like a great stinky turd, which was very appropriate as there were nasty brown liquid stains in the raccoon's grayish fur.

Gary couldn't help it; he bent over and threw up. Beside him, Sara did the same thing. And then, both wiping their mouths with the back of the hand, they stood and watched the raccoon emerge from the dead young woman's backside.

"Shoot it before it gets away," Sara whispered.

"I can't, not until it's completely outside of your friend."

"What the hell does that matter? She's already fucking dead. And she's not my friend; bitch tried to kill me."

Gary didn't reply. Once more he was holding his gun at the ready, waiting for this surreal occurrence to end. He really doubted that he could shoot Elvis anyway, and was trying to figure out another way to subdue the creature.

I got a couple of cages in the back of my truck, but how'm I gonna restrain Elvis long enough to cage him?

CHAPTER 29

"This is just so sickening to watch," Sara said as a smell of excrement polluted the morning.

Meanwhile, Elvis seemed to have gotten stuck inside Tess's rectum. Gary did not understand how this was possible, seeing as the raccoon's head and shoulders (which were obviously the widest part of its body) were already free, but he could not deny what he was seeing; Elvis was visibly squirming around in Tess's butthole, twisting and turning his body as if his lower limbs had gotten tangled up in the dead woman's intestines or his tail had knotted itself around her vertebral column.

"This is just absurd," Sara said. "It looks like it's being cut in half by her ass."

Gary and Sara watched Elvis's vain attempt to free himself for a while; but it was clearly no use, the raccoon was stuck.

Gary figured that even at this impasse, Elvis might have wrenched himself free of the sphincter trap, except that he insisted on holding onto the package of orange rock he'd become addicted to. Tightly gripping the pack of Agent Orange, he stared around him like he was confused and now and then hissed at Gary and Sara like they were responsible for his predicament, and continued his futile attempt to get free of his prior hidey hole.

"Look," Sara said after a few minutes had passed, "we can't stay here watching your little friend forever. So, are you going to shoot it or not? If you don't feel up to it, give me the gun and I'll shoot it."

"Oh yeah, alright I'll do it," Gary said grudgingly. Then he stepped up and carefully aimed the muzzle of his pistol at Elvis's little head. To do this though, he had to keep well out of way of the racoon's madly slavering jaws as it tried to bite him.

"Bye, little buddy," he said sadly, and then, avoiding looking into Elvis's crazy orange eyes, he pulled the gun's trigger, blowing the killer raccoon's head to a million pieces.

He found it sadly amusing that even as the raccoon died, he was still clenching on tightly to the pack of orange crack.

"Okay, so now that's taken care of," Gary said. "Time to get the boys in blue over here. Wincing, he pointed down at the headless animal stuck in the dead prostitute's behind. "But what everyone is going to make of this, I have no idea."

CHAPTER 30

As Gary had suspected, the police were even more surprised than he had been. At final count, they had seven corpses to collect, that number being completed by two bodies found just off the west trail, these latter pair of dead people being identified as brother and sister-in-law to the sole survivor's boyfriend.

The police had a hard time accepting that four of these corpses had been killed by a little raccoon, and not something larger, like a bear. Their skepticism concerning this was so intense that Gary wished he'd resisted blowing off Elvis's head, just so these legal non-believers could have seen the crazy creature's orange eyes for themselves. (The fragments of shattered raccoon head that forensics did recover weren't much proof, as the bullet that had killed Elvis had completely pulverized his eyes.) But at least they had been treated to the surreal sight of a woodland animal stuck half-in half-out of a woman's body.

The police took Sara to the station for questioning, and once they'd taken down her statement, released her to go home.

Finally, shaking his head at the whole mess, Gary drove home to Charlotte, who'd already watched the story of the killings on the news.

So, life in the Bentley household went on as normal. Despite Elvis's lethal misbehavior, however, Charlotte still staunchly refused to repent from her habit of feeding the raccoons. Gary finally decided it wasn't worth arguing over, and let her be.

Also, on Charlotte's request, he asked to be given Elvis's body for burial once forensics were through with it.

The body was handed over to him a week later, and Gary and Charlotte held a small funeral ceremony for Elvis, burying the raccoon at his favorite spot, beneath their house's front porch.

And this might have been the end of the story, but for the fact that for ages after that Gary kept being bothered by the suspicion that Elvis might come back from the dead and resume killing people again.

"Just so long as it's not campers next time," he told Charlotte one night. "That damn thieving little raccoon should just take its ass down to Las Vegas for its comeback."

The End

ABOUT THE AUTHOR

Gary Lee Vincent was born in Clarksburg, West Virginia and is an accomplished author, musician, actor, producer, director and entrepreneur. In 2010, his horror novel *Darkened Hills* was selected as 2010 Book of the Year winner by *Foreword Reviews Magazine* and became the pilot novel for *DARKENED - THE WEST VIRGINIA VAMPIRE SERIES*, that encompasses the novels *Darkened Hills, Darkened Hollows, Darkened Waters, Darkened Souls, Darkened Minds* and *Darkened Destinies.*

He has also authored the bizarro thriller *Passageway,* a tribute to H.P. Lovecraft, *When the Bedposts Shake,* an erotic horror, *THE BLACK CIRCLE CHRONICLES,* a five-part mini-series that includes the books, *Prove Your Love, Strange New Powers, Night Wings, Sheep Amongst Wolves,* and *Lord of the Birds.*

Gary co-authored the novel *Belly Timber* with John Russo, Solon Tsangaras, Dustin Kay and Ken Wallace, and co-authored the novel *Attack of the Melonheads* with Bob Gray and Solon Tsangaras.

As an actor, Gary has appeared in over a hundred feature films, including *Faded Memories, Midnight,* and *My Uncle John is a Zombie,* and multiple television series, including *House of Cards*, *Mindhunter*, *The Walking Dead*, and *Stranger Things*.

As a director, Gary got his directorial debut with *A Promise to Astrid*. He has also directed the films *Desk Clerk*, *Dispatched*, *Midnight*, *Godsend*, *Strange Friends*, and *Shoulder Down: Road to Redemption*.

OTHER GREAT TITLES FROM

Burning Bulb
PUBLISHING

WWW.BURNINGBULBPUBLISHING.COM

"Lots of action!" — Kimberly Bennett
Author, *Twisted Delight*

GARY LEE VINCENT

PASSAGEWAY

"This is a book that will keep you intrigued to the very end!"
—Christine Soltis, Author *Final Moon*

IMPOUND

GARY LEE VINCENT

GARY LEE VINCENT'S
DARKENED
THE WEST VIRGINIA VAMPIRE SERIES

DARKENED HILLS

When evil descends on a small West Virginia town, who will survive?

Jonathan did not start out his life to become a rambler, it justworked out that way. William was a troubled youth with something to hide. Both were from Melas, a small town tucked away in the West Virginia hills... a town where disappearances are happening more and more frequently.

After the suicide of a wanted serial killer, the townsfolk thought the nightmare was over. But when a centuries-old vampire is discovered they find out the hard way it's just getting started. Dark secrets can only stay hidden for so long and when the devil comes to collect, there will be hell to pay. Can Jonathan and William find a way to stop the vampire before it's too late? Find out in *Darkened Hills!*

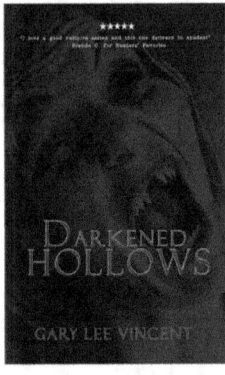

DARKENED HOLLOWS

In the heart-stopping sequel to the award-winning *Darkened Hills*, Jonathan and William must return to West Virginia to face possible criminal charges stemming from their last visit to the damned town of Melas, where both had narrowly escaped the clutches of a vampire seethe.

And as livestock start mysteriously getting murdered with all of their blood drained, worried farmers are searching for answers - leaving the local Sheriff and his deputy racing against time to learn the cause before a more violent crime is committed.

WWW.DARKENEDHILLS.COM

GARY LEE VINCENT'S
DARKENED
THE WEST VIRGINIA VAMPIRE SERIES

DARKENED WATERS

When the world goes to hell, the chosen must arise!

As Talman Cane orchestrates a flood of epic proportions in this third installment of the *Darkened* series the towns of Melas and Tarklin are caught completely off guard by the deluge. Hell-bent on finishing what they started, the evil brothers return to the lunatic asylum to take care of the witnesses and add to the ever-growing army of the undead.

Aided by Lucifer himself and the insane vampire demon Legion, the stage is set to channel all of the forces of hell to come forth. In an all-out race to survive, Jonathan, William, and Amanda soon discover they are up against impossible odds as Lucifer opens the Gateway to Hell, ushering in the zombie apocalypse and the End Times.

Find out who will survive this cosmic battle of the ages in *Darkened Waters!*

DARKENED SOULS

Melas and the Madison House are about to be rebuilt.
True evil is about to be reborne!

Young ex-priest and vampire-killer William is drawn back to the West Virginian town that almost killed him, where his vampire arch-enemy Victor Rothenstein still stalks the earth.

The town of Melas lies destroyed after the battle of the End of Days. But why is wealthy Jackie Nixon so eager to rebuild it using the bone dust of murdered souls?

Terrible evil has visited before, but the Gateway to Hell is about to be reopened in a horrific climax. And this time – it's personal.

www.DarkenedHills.com

GARY LEE VINCENT'S
DARKENED
THE WEST VIRGINIA VAMPIRE SERIES

DARKENED MINDS

Jackie Nixon intends to become Vampire Queen, but at what blood-drenched cost?

In this continuation to the explosive infernal saga begun in Darkened Souls, newly-turned vampire Jackie Nixon is taking no prisoners. Accompanied by her daughter, Kate, and by the captive vampire lord Victor Rothenstein, Jackie Nixon explores the Darkness. There, she intends to rouse the slumbering vampire race, bound under an ancient curse, and with their help, rule the human world.

But there's a deadly threat to Jackie's plans. Not just William who is trying to stop her, but her own royal ambitions. If Jackie performs the ritual to wake the sleeping vampires the wrong way, she could instead free the Red Beast of Hell, an unspeakable evil that even the undead fear.

DARKENED DESTINIES

With over 45 people missing after Jackie Nixon's party, the mysteries surrounding Melas and the Madison House keep getting darker.

Now, with legions of vampires at her command, can anything or anyone stop her from gaining complete control over all mankind?

The final battle has begun! As the Vampire Queen ascends her throne and sets to unleash the full forces of darkness, the fate of all things good hangs in the balance.

Burning Bulb
PUBLISHING

WWW.DARKENEDHILLS.COM

WHEN THE
BEDPOSTS
SHAKE

An Erotic Terror

GARY LEE VINCENT

STRANGE
FRIENDS

GARY LEE VINCENT

PROVE YOUR LOVE

GARY LEE VINCENT

STRANGE NEW
POWERS

THE BLACK CIRCLE CHRONICLES - BOOK 2

GARY LEE VINCENT

NIGHT WINGS

THE BLACK CIRCLE CHRONICLES - BOOK 3

GARY LEE VINCENT

SHEEP AMONGST
WOLVES
THE BLACK CIRCLE CHRONICLES - BOOK 4

GARY LEE VINCENT

LORD OF THE
BIRDS
THE BLACK CIRCLE CHRONICLES - BOOK 5
GARY LEE VINCENT

From the Creator of DARKENED HILLS...

RIVER
A VAMPIRE'S NIGHTMARE

GARY LEE VINCENT

A Vampire's Nightmare Continues . . .

RIVER

BOOK 2 ICARUS

GARY LEE VINCENT

THE BLIND MELODY

GARY LEE VINCENT

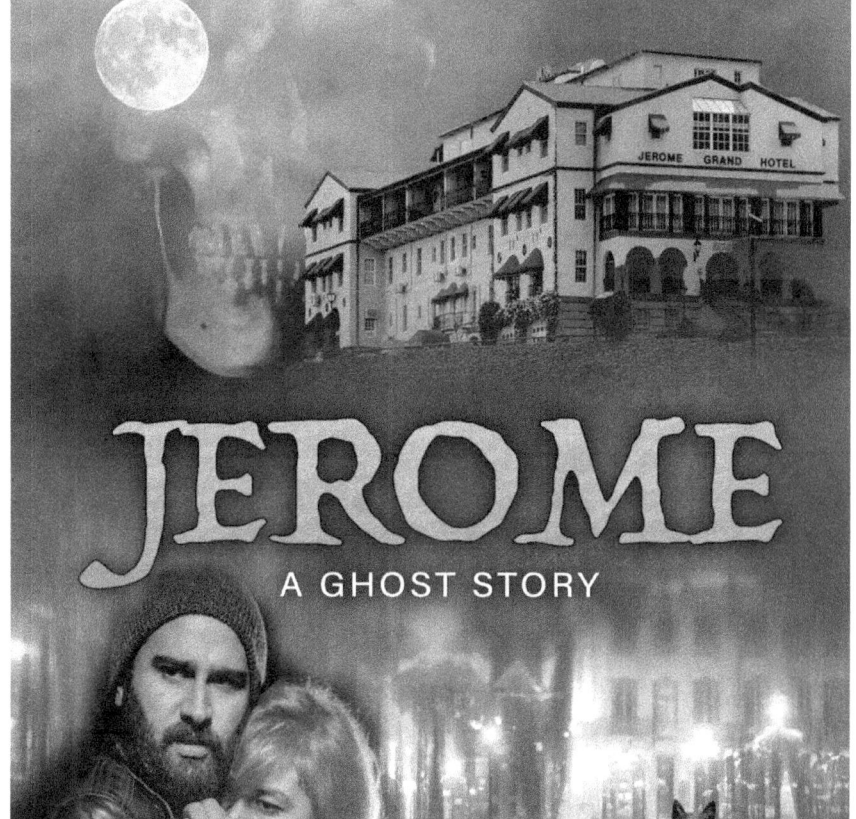

JEROME

A GHOST STORY

GARY LEE VINCENT

You've read the story, now witness the motion picture in all its blood-soaked glory from Director Brad Twigg!

For more information, visit
www.CRACKCOON.com